A Candlelight Ecstasy Romance®

"I REMEMBER COMING HOME, GETTING A BOTTLE, BUT I DON'T REMEMBER YOU—"

"Very flattering." Rana was so angry, she ached. She wondered why she'd been such a fool and how in the name of heaven she was going to get out of bed when the darned robe had come open and Luc was lying on half of it.

He looked down at her, his hand on his head. "We didn't—"

"No, we didn't," she said. "Your virtue is quite intact."

The pained look in his eyes gave way to amusement. "Is that why you're so angry?"

"I'm angry because I didn't expect to be here when you woke up. I'm angry because I was stupid enough to let a drunken cowboy sweet-talk me into bed."

"I wish I could remember how I did it."

"Well, I do remember," she shot back, "and believe me, it won't work twice."

CANDLELIGHT ECSTASY ROMANCES®

BALANCE OF POWER

Shirley Hart

Published by
Dell Publishing Co., Inc.
1 Dag Hammarskjold Plaza
New York, New York 10017

ISBN: 0-440-10382-7

Printed in the United States of America
First printing—December 1984

To Our Readers:

We have been delighted with your enthusiastic response to Candlelight Ecstasy Romances®, and we thank you for the interest you have shown in this exciting series.

In the upcoming months we will continue to present the distinctive, sensuous love stories you have come to expect only from Ecstasy. We look forward to bringing you many more books from your favorite authors and also the very finest work from new authors of contemporary romantic fiction.

As always, we are striving to present the unique, absorbing love stories that you enjoy most—books that are more than ordinary romance.

Your suggestions and comments are always welcome. Please write to us at the address below.

Sincerely,

The Editors
Candlelight Romances
1 Dag Hammarskjold Plaza
New York, New York 10017

CHAPTER ONE

The streets were like ovens. Heat radiated from everywhere, from the sky where the August sun shone down mercilessly, from the sides of the concrete buildings, from the cement beneath Rana O'Neill's feet. Her high heels snapped up and down in a staccato beat as she unwisely hurried along with the rest of New York's slightly wilted pedestrians toward her destination. She swerved inward, automatically avoiding the iron grids that were a trap for spike-heeled shoes. She shouldn't have worn heels, but she wasn't tall, only medium height in three-inch heels, and she needed the extra height to give her the confidence to face Clem.

Damn him! He wasn't her boss anymore, or her keeper, either. But her obligation to Clem would never be fully repaid. She owed him everything—including the fact that she wrote a syndicated column, which gave her the unique freedom to tell him to jump in the river if she felt like it.

Her slim body moved quickly through the crowd with an agility that stemmed from long practice rather than grace. She had walked to the *Sun Star* office for many years, and even though she hadn't done it recently, the route and the technique came back to her. She executed a neatly timed sidestep to avoid having the jean-clad mime in whiteface press a "yer into her hand and circled around the banana and grape stand planted on the corner. In the heat, the fruit looked overripe, used.

She longed for the coolness of her apartment, muttered a few choice words about Clem under her breath, and pushed back a lock of cinnamon-brown hair that clung to her damp forehead.

If it weren't for him, she would still be home sleeping, her body nude and cool under the blue sheet. But no, because Clem wanted to see her, here she was, out on the street with the other two tenths of the world's population that had collectively lost its mind and was trying to fry itself to death.

The *Sun Star* building was air-conditioned, but in the near hundred-degree heat the system was taxed to the limit. Even so, when the revolving door spilled her into the interior of the building, she sighed with sheer delight as the cooler air touched her skin.

She walked past the heavily draped floor-to-ceiling glass walls and went up the half flight of stairs that led to the elevator. Impatiently, she punched the up button and stepped back, her teeth catching her lower lip. How much cooler the temperature would be when she got to Clem's office was questionable. And she didn't have to guess what he wanted to see her about. She knew Clem was a longtime friend of Lucas Garrett's. And she had flayed Garrett alive in her column yesterday.

The elevator doors opened, and she moved forward slightly, just as some clumsy oaf of a man stepped out of the car . . . and walked sideways into her.

He nearly knocked the breath out of her, and his clodhopper foot came down hard on one of her toeless shoes. She felt the air leave her lungs, felt the sharp sting of tears in her eyes. She grasped her shoulder bag instinctively, although whether she suspected him of trying to steal it, or whether she had planned to hit him with it, she wasn't sure.

She opened her mouth to say something sharp. His head swiveled around, and his eyes looked into hers. Her normally quick tongue failed her.

"I'm sorry," he said. "I didn't see you."

She ducked her head. "It's all right," she mumbled and stepped into the elevator. Reluctantly, knowing she must, she turned around and faced the front. He was still standing where she'd left him, but now recognition flared in his eyes, recognition—and anger.

"Wait!" he shouted. "I want to talk to you."

He reached out, trying to delay the closing of the door. She gave him a quick shove backward. "Darling, I'm in a hurry. I'll talk to you later . . . at the apartment." She smiled sweetly and lifted her hand to wave at him as the doors slid noiselessly closed. There was a curious murmur from the people in the car as it glided upward. One of the women smiled at Rana. She smiled back and expelled the breath of air she'd been holding. She had just called Lucas Garrett, a man she'd dissected in this morning's column but had never before seen, "darling," and she'd practically done him bodily harm. He must be furious.

What was he doing in the *Sun Star* building? Or did she even have to guess?

When she walked into the office of the editor in chief, Clem rose from behind the desk in old-fashioned courtesy.

Sir Galahad . . . but when he sits down, he'll fry my hide.

Even without fire in his eye, Clem was impressive. He was a massive man who'd been told by his doctor at least five times in the last two years to get his weight down. When she was seated, he grunted and sat down in his swivel chair. It was an old wooden one, a relic from his days with the *Indiana News,* and it creaked alarmingly when he leaned back in it and folded his hands behind his head. "You've stirred up a damn hornet's nest with this column, Rana."

"I'm fine," she said evenly. "How are you, Clem?"

He dropped his hands from behind his head and picked up the newspaper that lay open on his desk.

"Why the hell did you write it?"

She met his gaze steadily. "Because it's the truth. Lucas T. Garrett is a male chauvinist."

"But did you have to say this?" He stabbed his finger at the printed page.

"Which?" she asked politely, one sable-brown brow raised in inquiry as she smiled at him.

"That his books ought to be"—he pushed his glasses up on his nose and read—" 'labeled by the Surgeon General as haz-

11

ardous to your health.' " Clem laid the paper down and stared at her over the top of his half glasses. "Don't you know people have been sued for less?"

"Garrett isn't going to sue me, Clem. I write an opinion column."

"That doesn't make you immune," he snorted.

She smiled at him. "Why worry? Your paper's not responsible for me anymore. I'm syndicated. I'll be the one who'll get sued, not you."

"I've got too much time and trouble invested in you to see you lose your readership because you are involved in litigation."

"Clem, you worry too much."

"You young people don't worry enough."

Rana looked at him steadily. "He's a friend of yours, isn't he?"

Clem studied her through eyes that had narrowed. "Yes."

"And you want me to lay off."

"Yes."

Those quiet words would have struck terror into the heart of any hardened reporter, but Rana shook her head. "What kind of a syndicated columnist would I be if I let you dictate terms to me?"

Without blinking an eye, Clem said, "A sensible one."

She smiled. "Well, that lets me out then. You know that's one thing I'm not."

He smiled slightly, and the effect was as frightening as his frown. He had the look of a cobra contemplating dinner. "You're taking on more than you can handle with Luc, Rana."

She brought her palms down on the leather arms of his chair, slapping them in a fair imitation of Clem in more amiable moments, and got to her feet. "I consider myself warned. Now, if you don't mind, I'd like to go home. I've got a column to write."

"Home." Clem eyed her owlishly. "That place where you live

12

isn't a home. It's an overnight rest stop for the upwardly mobile."

"Thank you," she said sweetly, thinking at this point that discretion was the better part of valor.

"If you had a man, you'd get some comfortable furniture, and you'd relax. You wouldn't find it necessary to attack the first man who comes down the pike who is a real man and not some pussyfooting Wall Street dandy who—"

"Clem," she warned, "we've known each other for a long time, ever since you saved me from starvation ten years ago. I want to go on being your friend. Please stop saying these things to me just to relieve your dyspepsia. I like my apartment, and I don't need a man." She didn't exactly talk through her teeth, but the strength and the grit were there, and he knew it.

Clem stared at her. "If I get a phone call from Luc—"

"Refer him to me," she said over her shoulder, wanting badly to ask him if Luc had preceded her into the office, but knowing it wouldn't do any good if she did. Clem was a master at asking questions, but he didn't answer anything.

"You bet I will." Clem's voice followed her out the door.

She went home and tried to work, but Clem had struck a nerve and destroyed her power of concentration. She got up from the computer table and looked around, a frown drawing her brows together over her nose. All right, so there wasn't anything of permanence in her apartment. She wanted it that way. She wanted to be able to pick up and move at any moment. She wanted to be free of traditions, free of possessions, free of memories. . . .

There was nothing wrong with her apartment. The floor was covered with a creamy beige wall-to-wall rug that was soft and fluffy and invited sprawling. She'd covered wooden boxes with the same carpeting and scattered bright, jewel-colored pillows around on the floor. She had a small portable television set perched on one of the boxes, and on another there was a tea set. There was nothing in her apartment of permanence, nothing of her. That was what Clem objected to.

He had come to see her once. He had perched his oversized body on one of her carpet-covered blocks, and he had looked like a comic statue sold in a novelty shop. All he needed were the words "I wuv you" painted at his feet. He'd hated her decor, and he told her so, outright. He hadn't brought it up again until this morning.

She gave one of the giant pillows a futile kick. What did she care what Clem thought? Her apartment was exactly the way she wanted it. It contained nothing that couldn't be moved or left if she had the urge to pick up and go.

Around six o'clock she gave up the unproductive task of trying to pull words from her mind and got ready for her evening with Philip. She dressed, humming under her breath, looking forward to several hours of conversation in which the name of Mr. Garrett would not arise. But when she went to the door to admit Phil, he scraped over the same sensitive nerve end.

"Your column today was a little strong—even for you, sweetheart," he said, bending over and brushing her cheek with his lips. Phil worked on Wall Street and had the air of money about him. Not that he was overly generous with it. She paid for his dinner almost as often as he paid for hers.

"Et tu, Brutus?" she said lightly, holding out her arms for him to place the lacy black shawl over her shoulders. She wore a bronzed coppery dress that shimmered and shone beneath the shawl except where her bare shoulders gleamed through.

"I take it you've been criticized from other quarters?" She'd piled her hair up on top of her head, and his mouth brushed the nape of her neck. Phil was urbanely restrained. It was typical of him to kiss her while he talked about her column. He seemed to hold her hand, dance with her, and brush his lips over hers at the end of an evening almost out of habit. He'd been married before, and she often wondered if he realized he was out with her and not his former wife.

"Drawn and quartered is more like it."

Phil laughed softly. "Clem after your hide, is he?"

"He's developed a taste for me, I think."

"I can understand that. I've developed a taste for you, myself."

They were out in the hall by then, and he was shepherding her to the elevator. She shot him a startled look, but he merely pushed her inside and leaned forward to punch the first-floor button. Phil rarely indulged in sexual repartee, and the fact that he had disturbed her. She wasn't in the mood for fencing with another prowling male, not tonight. That's why she'd allowed Phil to get close to her, because he'd seemed so uninterested in her as a woman.

Phil chatted casually to her in the cab, only taking her hand when the taxi pulled up in front of the Tavern-on-the-Green and they were forced to wait for one of the horse-drawn hansom cabs to make a circle in front of them. The cabbie muttered darkly at the other driver, but he had no choice but to wait for the slower vehicle to turn.

When the horse clopped away, the cab drew up to the door. They went inside and were shown to one of the tables along the brass railing. The waiter held her chair for her and handed her the menu.

They were enjoying a cocktail when a couple was seated at the table directly across the railing from them.

How many millions of people were there in New York? Six? Seven? And how many restaurants? Thousands? But out of those thousands of dining places, few were as well known as the Tavern-on-the-Green. And few would have attracted Lucas T. Garrett and his date.

She had known he was in town even before he'd knocked her breathless and tromped on her foot. He was here promoting his latest book. He'd been on that famous late night talk show the week before last, and he'd charmed the normally acerbic female host to distraction. Rana had watched with gritted teeth and then gone to her word processor and written her column. That was her first mistake.

No, not a mistake, she thought fiercely. His books were just what she had said, male chauvinist statements that portrayed women as rewards for a man's valor. They were filled with the worst kind of romanticizing. It annoyed her. Garrett was a fine writer, but his attitude toward women marred his work. And that's what she'd said in her column.

Now, seated at an angle across from her, his soft, velvety drawl was as audible as the steady beat of her heart. She'd put down all that biographical hype the publisher had put out about Garrett being born and brought up on a ranch in Wyoming as so much propaganda. But there he was, big as life, sitting down in the chair facing hers, his height putting him high enough to be seen over the railing. He wore a dark blue western-cut suit and a Kentucky colonel tie, glittery silver strings that accented the tanned tautness of his throat, and he was acting the part of a western gentleman for all he was worth. The soft velvet of his voice fell like honey on her ear.

The woman he was with lapped up every syrupy word. The sound of her husky, feminine laughter grated on Rana's nerves. Rana's teeth clicked together, her food forgotten.

Rana lowered her head, but it wasn't necessary. Garrett didn't see her at all. He had eyes only for his companion. He, on the other hand, filled the view in front of her to the exclusion of everything else, his eyes as blue as the sparkling stained-glass circle that hung on the wall behind his head. His voice, too, captured her attention. She found herself wishing Phil would stop talking so that she could hear what Garrett was saying.

She couldn't hear his words. All she could hear with any real clarity was the sound of his companion's intimate laughter coming in frequent little bursts.

He must be very good company.

It was rotten bad luck that Rana had to sit there and listen to them, and it was even worse luck that, as she was finishing her meal, a woman stepped into the aisle, whipped a camera out of her purse, and stood at just the right angle to get both Rana and Lucas Garrett in focus. Damn! A reporter! Rana moved, but a click told her she hadn't dodged soon enough. At the same time Lucas Garrett's eyes found hers. He looked from Rana to the

16

woman, who was now tucking her camera into her purse with a self-satisfied smile. His eyes were as blue and stormy as the western skies he wrote about.

"Garnering publicity, Ms. O'Neill?"

Of course he recognized her. After the incident that morning, he wouldn't be likely to forget her.

Furious, she said, "I might ask you the same thing, Mr. Garrett."

The photographer's camera clicked again, this time from Lucas Garrett's side of the railing. Garrett's eyes went icy, and his head swung around. Rana felt a fleeting relief that it was the woman photographer who was the source of his attention now and not her. Philip looked at Rana. Always urbane, he said easily, "I think this might be a good time to leave, don't you?"

Rana hated retreat, but in the interest of avoiding a scene in an elegant restaurant, she said, "I think that's an excellent idea." Her dress rustled as she slid out of the chair. Her head high, she didn't see Lucas Garrett wave the woman photographer away so that he could watch Rana go.

Her enjoyment in the evening was gone, and Phil knew it. He was silent in the cab. At the door, he gave her a light kiss and said, "Sorry, honey. Maybe we'll have better luck this weekend."

"Come here to the apartment Saturday night," she said impulsively, breaking her ironclad rule. "We'll dine in."

Philip held her in his arms but pulled away from her to look into her face. "Are you sure?"

"I'm sure."

Even after she had opened the door and went into the apartment, it wasn't the quizzical gaze of Phil's eyes she remembered. It was the look of blazing anger in Lucas Garrett's that burned itself into her memory.

The next day her streak of bad luck continued. She forgot about Lucas Garrett, forgot about the column she had written about him. The relentless press of new deadlines took all her attention. She wrote all morning, but nothing seemed right. The words were stiff, unbending. Ideas eluded her. Her mind was blank.

Aching for something to look at besides the little green letters on her computer screen, she had agreed to meet her girl friend Kris for lunch in the Sungarden Lounge at the Hyatt. Then, as if the writing devil had planned it, she had a string of good ideas. She sat down at the computer again and wrote, unconscious of time passing until she jumped up, looked at the clock, and realized she'd have to rush like crazy to get ready. She got out of her jeans and put on the yellow sundress that bared her shoulders, and left her hair loose. She struggled into nylons, grabbed the first pair of high-heeled sandals she could find, and flew out the door. It wasn't until she was in the cab that she noticed the heel on one of her shoes was wobbly. She got out of the cab carefully and tread lightly as she and Kris walked up the marble stairs, but after she had eaten in the midst of the marble and glass and plant life with the sound of water tumbling off the flat marble surface and Kris's chatter filling her ears, and they got up to go, she looked down into the lobby area below and saw the dark brown head of Lucas Garrett. He was with a different woman this time, a stunning, older redhead dressed in a vivid lime-green suit, a woman she vaguely recognized as being part of the publishing world. Lucas Garrett was listening to her, his head bent. Anxious to get away, she started down the stairs ahead of Kris.

Garrett's head swiveled round, and at the same time, on the third step from the bottom, her heel twisted. She careened down the rest of the stairs, groping for something, anything, to stop her fall. What stopped her was the hard chest of a warm male body.

He stood with one foot ahead of the other to brace himself for her weight, and now he took the full brunt of her fall, his hands catching her just under her breasts. Head reeling, breath knocked from her, she came to an abrupt stop against his hard chest. As she tried to regain her equilibrium, he supported her through the aftershock of her fall, wrapping both arms around her to steady her.

Her senses stopped whirling, only to be dazzled by the scent and feel of the man who held her. He turned her more fully into his arms so that she rested against his lean length, chest against breast, hip against hip. The suede western suit he wore was the color of carmel candy and soft as a glove, but beneath the softness a man's hard body flared to life.

Awareness flooded her veins.

She pushed herself away from him, but he didn't let her go. She stood with his arms wrapped around her and felt foolish and stupid. One tumble into Lucas Garrett's arms had destroyed every bit of her hard-won adult sophistication. She felt like a clumsy five-year-old with warm cheeks and tousled hair.

He recognized her at once; she could see that. How could he not? This was the second time in as many days they'd met head on.

"Now this is a little more to my liking," he said. "Stairs *are* better than elevators."

"Don't"—she struggled, trying to tear away from him—"be ridiculous."

Mere inches away from her mouth, his lips curved. His eyes cataloged each strand in the loose cloud of cinnamon-brown hair that floated around her shoulders. The expression in those blue depths annoyed her. "Is that what I'm being?" he said softly.

"Let me go." The whisper that should have come out in anger sounded husky and disturbed.

He moved his hips, accomplishing the impossible task of pressing her closer and added insult to injury by murmuring, "I couldn't do that, now, could I? I have my male chauvinist reputation to uphold."

He shifted slightly, and her face burned with heat. She pushed herself away from his supporting arm—and this time he let her go. She stepped back, and, forgetting her broken heel, lost her balance and nearly fell again.

His hard hand found her elbow once more. He pulled her upright and said in an amused tone, "You *can* stand on your own two feet, can't you?"

Furious, she tugged her arm free of his grasp. "Of course I can."

"Lucas?" The woman behind him sounded amused. "Is this someone you know?"

"Patrice, this is Rana O'Neill."

"Ah," said Patrice, her eyes gleaming. "That Rana O'Neill. The lady who doesn't like your books."

Rana bristled. "I didn't say I didn't like his books. It's his women I don't like."

"What's the matter with Lucas's women?" She sounded genuinely interested.

"They're stereotyped . . . rewards to the hero for good behavior."

"I think I should warn you that Patrice is my editor," Lucas Garrett said, his eyes moving lazily over Rana.

Rana closed her eyes. To the red-haired woman she said, "I'm sorry. I didn't mean—"

"But of course you did," Patrice said, her eyes sparkling. "I find your views extremely interesting, especially since you're the first one who has ever found anything to criticize in Lucas's books."

"Well, that makes me the minority of one, I guess."

"Lucas does write about another era and men's attitudes were a little different back during the days our country was being settled," Patrice said reasonably.

"I realize that. I . . ." Rana's eyes slid over his western clothes. She could see why he was at home writing about the past. In the ultramodern marble cavern of the Hyatt lobby, he looked out of time, a man from another era, a pirate in command, a brown-haired Viking raider. That lazily assessing gaze should have disappeared with the slave auction block.

Patrice said, "Lucas was telling me about your column. You write opinion, I believe he said." Her green eyes moved over

20

Rana's face as if she was searching for something. "Being syndicated, you have a large audience. Don't you think you have a responsibility to your readers to deal fairly with the books and authors you discuss?"

"His books are excellent. Only his women are objectionable."

"Using your opinion column to air your views seems to be just a bit . . . unfair," Patrice said coolly. "Lucas has no place to print a rebuttal."

Rana's eyes flashed while she smiled sweetly at Lucas. "I have an idea of how you can avenge yourself on me, Mr. Garrett. Put me in your next book. I'm sure I'll recognize myself. I'll be the villainess who corrupts a poor but honest cowboy and drives him to a life of degradation as a cattle rustler."

"Don't tempt me." He sounded amused.

"That would be the day, wouldn't it?" she shot back, not thinking.

"Yes, it certainly would." Heavy with sensual teasing, his drawl poured over her.

Sunlight flickered on his brown hair, giving it a red sheen. Or was she just seeing red?

Kris said something under her breath, her eyes moving upward. Rana was suddenly aware that a group had gathered at the top of the stairs and were looking at them curiously. In New York, where everyone scrupulously minded their own business, she had made yet another scene with Mr. Lucas Garrett. All she needed was the woman reporter with her blasted camera to make the scenario complete.

Oh, well. Might as well make it a good one. She reached down and took off her shoe. The broken heel dangled awkwardly in her hand as she turned to Kris. "Let's get out of here."

She teetered away on the nylon-covered toe and one high-heeled shoe and was almost to the revolving door when Lucas Garrett's voice rose to the high ceiling of the Hyatt's lobby.

"Oh, Ms. O'Neill."

She gritted her teeth and turned. "Yes?"

He paused. "Nice to . . . run into you again."

A man at the top of the stairs laughed. How did he do it? How did he remind her of those few seconds in his arms with just words? The sexual teasing was unmistakable in the low voice that carried to every corner of the multilevel room.

She said a word under her breath, whirled around, and pushed on the revolving door.

They couldn't get a taxi right away, of course, and a sensation on the back of her neck made her skin crawl. She twisted to look up. He was there, seated in the sun-room. He faced the street and the glass wall gave him a full view of her. He waved cheerily.

She was so desperate to escape him that she ran out into the traffic to accost the next taxi that came along. Her flashing eyes intimidated even the driver, and he let them in.

"He ought to be an actor with that timing and delivery," she muttered to Kris in the taxi a few minutes later.

Kris's eyes were wide. "Why didn't you introduce me? I was dying. He is gorgeous. Lucas Garrett. Oh, my God, I've wanted to meet him since I read his first book."

"Well, just stay with me. With my luck I'll probably run into him again tomorrow before I get out of bed."

"Now there's an idea."

Rana grimaced.

Kris laughed. "Have you been running into him a lot lately?"

"I seem to be."

Kris let out a breath. "If you guarantee you'll meet him tomorrow, I'll follow you like a shadow."

"I have a better idea. Why don't you just call up his publisher and ask for his itinerary? He's in New York all this week peddling his book."

The irony was lost on Kris. She twisted around to look back at the Hyatt through the window of the cab as if she could see Garrett. "I'm going to buy a copy tonight after work. Maybe he'll autograph it for me."

Rana raised her eyebrow. "Some friend you are. Didn't you read my review?"

"Sure I did. But you're inclined to go off the deep end."

In sudden silence in the cab, Rana twisted to look at Kris, her face paling. Kris rushed to undo the damage. "I mean, that's why your readers read you. They love you. You give them that daring sense of freedom because you always go just a little further than you should . . . I mean . . ."

"I think you'd better quit while you're ahead, friend."

"Oh, Rana. You know your column is outrageous. Who else but you could accuse one of the best-selling authors in the world of being a male chauvinist? I mean, obviously he isn't. If he was, no woman would buy one of his books." Her rush of words stopped, and she frowned. "Would she?"

"That's just my point. Women do buy his books."

"And you think they shouldn't."

"I didn't say that. My purpose isn't to discourage anybody from buying books. I'd be a fool to do that. My purpose is to get people to think about the books that they are buying. Instead of just mindlessly buying a book because it's been called a best seller, I want them to know a little something about the book and the author so they can decide if it's right for them. Is that wrong?"

Kris shook her sleek blond head. "No, of course not . . . as long as you don't air your personal gripes."

Exasperated, Rana cut in, "Of course I air my personal gripes. That's what the column is—my opinion."

Kris turned to look at her, her brown eyes troubled. "Then don't jump all over me for merely stating mine. I think Lucas Garrett is adorable."

Rana let out a long breath. "Of course he's adorable. That's not the point. The point is, he doesn't portray women as real people in his books. They are idealized sex objects."

"I wonder why."

"My guess is it's because that's the only kind of woman he's ever known, the kind of woman he feels comfortable with. He's

23

noted for his affairs. He's never had a real relationship with a woman. He doesn't know what it's like to just talk to a woman."

"Talk?" Kris sank back against the car seat. "What woman in her right mind would want to talk to him if he was in the mood for . . . something else? Rana, be sensible. He can be my idealized sex object any day."

Rana stared at her and shook her head. "That's crazy. You don't even know him. You look at him and you think . . ." Her eyes widened. "That's it! He isn't able to see a woman as anything more than a sex object because that's the way a woman sees him."

Kris rolled her eyes. "I'd look at him any way he wanted me to—upside down, sideways . . ."

"Would you really?" Rana stared in front of her, thinking.

The cab pulled up in front of Kris's office building. Kris sat up and gave Rana a peeved look. "Do you know why the whole world hates writers?"

"No, why?"

"Because they go into trances when you talk to them, and they don't have to go back to the office after lunch."

"Hey." Rana made an effort to pull her mind away from the ideas that were swirling through it. She smiled at Kris. "You had your chance to try free-lancing a couple of years before you started writing ad copy."

Kris eyed her. "Deciding between free-lancing and eating is not a choice. Give me a call soon, okay?"

Rana nodded absently. Her mind was already racing. She was writing a column.

Kris turned her back to Rana and scrambled out of the cab. To the cabbie, she said, "Watch her. When she gets that glazed look in her eyes, she's writing in her head. Better get her to tell you her destination before she forgets where she's going."

The cabbie was unshockable. "Yeah, sure."

She mumbled her address, annoyed at being dragged out of her thoughts. When the cab pulled up in front of her apartment building, she paid the fare, hardly able to contain her impatience to get at her computer.

The next morning the phone rang, waking Rana. She pulled her pillow over her head. The phone went on ringing. One bare arm reached out from under the sheet and brought the receiver to her ear under the pillow.

"Hello."

A feminine voice said stiffly in her ear, "Thanks a lot."

Rana came awake. "Kris? What's the matter?"

"I just read your column." Kris's voice was icy.

Rana scrambled upward, fighting to the surface above the sheet and pillow. "And?"

"Is that the way you see me?"

"See you? I don't know what you're talking about."

" 'The saying goes that beauty is in the eye of the beholder,' " Kris read from Rana's column, her voice dry and cool. " 'But what of the beheld?' " Rana moaned and fought the urge to stuff the pillow in her ears and refuse to listen.

Kris stopped reading. "Did you say something?"

"Too damn much," Rana muttered.

"Isn't that the truth." There was a grim satisfaction in her words. "I'm just getting to the good part. 'To look at a person and react to their attractiveness is possibly the ultimate in selfishness. We think only of ourselves, and in so doing, encourage the object of our admiration to think only of himself. We spread selfishness like an oil slick. We breathe it into the air, we scatter it like confetti. It's an infectious thing, selfishness. We spread it like a contagious disease, and then we go away, leaving the celebrity empty, unfulfilled—a hollow god seeking a new admirer to bring the luster back to the gold shell.' "

Kris stopped reading. Rana waited, her head aching. Kris said, "Underneath all that fancy imagery, I get the feeling you're trying to tell me something. Something about myself and Lucas Garrett. Something about my selfishness."

"Kris, I didn't have you specifically in mind. I was thinking about the reaction he gets from any woman, all women."

"But it was my conversation that sparked this column."

"Yes, but . . ." Rana trailed helplessly into silence, at a loss for a way to explain. The quiet from the other end was ominous.

Kris said, "You want to know what I think? I think you're jealous."

The words stabbed. She said coolly, "Don't be absurd."

Kris made a sound that should have been a laugh but wasn't. "I was with you when you fell into his arms, remember? I saw your face."

"I don't even know the man."

"Didn't you tell me once you wrote from the unconscious, illogical, right side of your brain?"

Rana sighed, knowing retribution was at hand. "I said something about it, yes."

"I suggest you try the other side," Kris said crisply, "the side that can put two and two together." The phone clicked in Rana's ear.

She hung up the receiver, feeling a sharp pang of regret. She'd known Kris for a long time. She'd consoled Kris through a divorce, rejoiced with Kris when she'd found another man who seemed to care for her very much. Yet now she seemed in danger of losing her friendship.

Why had she attacked Kris for finding Lucas Garrett attractive? Half the women in the world felt the same way. She wasn't jealous. She felt nothing for Lucas Garrett at all . . . except perhaps a regret for his waste of his own talent.

Later that day, while she munched on her solitary lunch of cottage cheese on a lettuce leaf, she thought about all the occupations she might have taken up, a sure sign that the writing was not going well. She took a look at her half-eaten lunch and realized her appetite was gone. She pitched the food into the garbage and went back to her computer to write another column, one she hoped would be the final one on the subject of Mr.

Lucas Garrett. She spent hours on it, as many as she could with the press of her deadline looming over her. When she read it over again, she still felt a vague dissatisfaction.

"We are all vulnerable," she had written. "We try to shield ourselves at every opportunity. Yet no writer can truly hide from his readers. Words on the page are a beacon into the mind.

"Mr. Garrett has made himself accessible to the media, thereby denying himself the shield of anonymity that most writers prefer. Perhaps he finds it necessary to hide in his writing, to create women that do not touch him emotionally. We should give him that right. No one should have to expose his soul to the entire world . . ." The telephone rang. Rana debated whether to answer. When the rings continued, she rose from her chair.

Her caller identified herself as an assistant producer of a daytime talk show that Rana knew discussed social issues.

"I'm calling to make arrangements for you to be on our show," the woman said brusquely.

"Who gave you my telephone number?" Rana said warily.

"We called the *Sun Star*, your old newspaper." The woman sounded faintly peeved that Rana had sidetracked her. "We want you to appear on our show with Mr. Garrett and discuss your ideas with him about the chauvinism you say he displays in his books. Now, what I need is a list of dates when you would be available. We'll match those with the list we get from Mr. Garrett, and then I'll get back to you on the dates the two of you have in common—"

"I'm sorry," Rana said coolly. "I won't appear on your show."

There was a silence, as if the woman had not expected to be refused and didn't have any pat phrases of rebuttal.

"Don't be ridiculous," her caller snapped at last. "You can't afford to hide your head in the sand. People are talking about your column and the things you've been saying. If you come on our show, the readership of your column will double."

"I'm not interested."

"Ms. O'Neill." The woman used the same tone she might have used if she were speaking to a child. "You have nothing to fear. We have one of the largest viewing audiences in the country, and our viewers have come to expect an in-depth survey of the topics we choose to discuss. Surely the truth can't harm you."

The subtle implication was there, creating a siren song. If she didn't come on the program, it was because she didn't really believe in the things she wrote. She ignored it. "I'm still not interested."

"You're turning down a great opportunity to—"

"—make a fool of myself," Rana finished flatly.

There was a pause. Then the cool, businesslike voice said, "I think you've managed to do that very efficiently yourself without any help from us."

"Well, it must be comforting to know that there are still some things left in this world that the Dave Hartley show is not responsible for." As a put down it was mild compared to what Rana would like to have said, but the woman's reaction was instant. The phone clicked in Rana's ear.

Her nerves on edge, she went back to the computer . . . and knew that she simply could not write another column for publication about Lucas Garrett. With precision, she picked up the printed sheets, tore them in half . . . and settled down to write another column that had been floating around in the back of her mind. She knew she would be there at the keyboard well into the night.

The rest of the day went by in a frantic spate of writing, telephone calls from people she knew, and people she had forgotten she knew. She was an instant celebrity. She prayed her return to oblivion would be as swift.

That night, when she finally went to bed in the wee hours, she had a nightmare. She dreamt she was poised on a high diving board far above a pool surrounded by a crowd of people. She bent and went flying into the air . . . and as she did, the shimmering blue water in the pool below disappeared and there

28

was nothing to stop her fall . . . nothing except the body of Lucas Garrett, clad in a three-piece suit. He stood on the ground below and waited for her with outstretched arms.

She came awake, drenched in her own perspiration. She got up and prowled restlessly, unable to sleep, knowing full well what the dream meant. She cursed herself for a fool, went out into her living room, and sat on one of her huge pillows with her legs crossed and drank black coffee. When she finished, she paced the floor restlessly, like a caged lion. At last, when the sun turned the sky to a faint pink, she went back into her bedroom and lay down on the bed.

When she woke the second time, the sounds of the city told her it was almost noon. The deep-seated restlessness washed over her again. She had to get some fresh air.

She showered and dressed quickly, getting into a light cotton dress made of India madras that had every shade of brown and tan imaginable in it and skimmed her body to tie over her shoulders with the narrowest of spaghetti straps. Open-toed sandals with no stockings left her feet and legs cool and bare. She caught her long brown hair back at the nape with a turquoise barrette.

She went into the hall and pressed the button for the elevator. A few minutes later, on the ground floor of her apartment building, she pushed open the door and emerged out onto the heated, noisy street, suddenly filled with an exhilarating sense of freedom. Two blocks from her apartment was a small coffee shop she frequented. She turned down the street and headed into the sunshine, glad to be out among the vigorous hustle and bustle of the city.

In the underground coffee shop, she returned Tom's smile, picked up her cup of coffee from the high counter, selected a doughnut, and slid into a high-backed booth, her back to the door.

From somewhere over her shoulder a familiar voice, slightly muffled, said, "I'll have a regular and two of those chocolate-covered doughnuts."

29

In the act of lifting her coffee to her lips, she froze. She turned. At the same moment, so did he. And through the one big window in front, sunlight glinted off that dark hair, highlighting the red fire. One elbow was draped against the counter. "Hello, Ms. O'Neill," he said, his eyes gleaming with amusement—and the cool, deliberate enjoyment of a hunter who has found his prey.

CHAPTER TWO

"This isn't a coincidence," Rana said flatly.

"Did you think it might be?" He held his cup of coffee and the doughnuts wrapped in a napkin in his hand and slid into the booth on the same side with her, using his body to nudge her over. Not a drop spilled out of his coffee cup. An instant memory charged through her, the memory of that hard body pressed against hers in the hotel lobby. The aroma of coffee and sweet pastry and good suede leather mingled together to tantalize her nose.

He laid the doughnuts on the table, his lean and capable hands spreading the napkin out, the fingers tugging the end of the paper toward her. "I bought an extra one for you."

"Thanks, but I have my own." She gestured toward the half-eaten morsel that lay in front of her, glad to take her eyes away from his profile and the evidence of his good grooming, the smoothness of his chin, the combed neatness of his brown hair. He wore the same suede suit he had been wearing the other day, but this time his shirt was a silky brown one that he had left unbuttoned at the neck. He looked open, approachable, and utterly relaxed, as if meeting her this way was the most natural thing in the world.

In contrast, her whole body was alive with tension. She told herself it was merely because she didn't know what to expect from him. Her own sense of justice told her he had every right to be furious with her . . . but he didn't seem to be angry. She watched him pick up the white cup and lift it to his mouth cautiously.

31

"How did you find out about this place?" It was inane, but some sense of self-preservation told her to play it cool. Perhaps she was jumping to conclusions, thinking that he had sought her out.

"I asked around." He set his coffee down and twisted slightly in the bench, bringing the full force of those blue eyes around to face her, an arm going up to slide along the bench behind her shoulder. "A good writer knows how to ask the right questions."

She couldn't argue with that.

"You are a good writer, Mr. Garrett."

"We agree on something, at least."

He said it with such droll self-mockery that she had to smile. She toyed with her spoon, her appetite gone.

He said, "Well?"

She looked up, her eyes meeting his. "Well . . . what?"

"I'm waiting." He leaned back against the booth.

Her clear gray eyes met his blue ones. "What . . . are you waiting for?"

"I'm waiting for the next phase of your courtship. Aren't you going to ask me out to dinner?"

"What?" Surprise made her voice rise a tone above its normal huskiness.

"When a woman is interested in a man in this enlightened day and age, she usually asks him out."

"I am not interested in you."

"Aren't you?" His amiable smile lifted his lips, but she sensed something a little more steely in his tone. "You've spent the greater part of the last few days discussing me in your column. You've followed me around town, contriving to bump into me on two occasions. I would say a great deal of your energy has been spent on getting my attention." He leaned forward. "You have my attention, Ms. O'Neill. All of it."

She fought down the anger that closed her throat at his cool statement that she had maneuvered those accidental meetings, knowing her denial would be futile. She had to convince him somehow that he was not the center of her universe. She braced herself to sound cool. "Do you have any idea how many columns I write in a year, Mr. Garrett?"

He paused, his eyes narrowing in mock speculation. "Three times a week, fifty-two weeks a year . . . I'd say you must write about one hundred and fifty-six columns . . . not counting time off for good behavior or vacation."

He had the number exactly right and had, of course, stolen the impact of her words, but she forged bravely on. "With that many columns to get out, I have to use any available topic I feel I can intelligently discuss."

Without blinking, he said silkily, "What makes you think you can intelligently discuss me?"

The question was soft—but pointed. There was flint in his voice, and his eyes had changed subtly, to a darker, more dangerous blue.

She met his challenge with her head lifted. "I didn't discuss you. I discussed your work."

"Your comments were aimed at me."

"You're a celebrity. You're public property. Anyone can discuss you . . . as long as what they say isn't an outright lie that will damage your career. And my guess is," she said, making a shrewd stab in the dark and watching him carefully to see the effect of her words, "that my columns have made your book sales go up, not down."

Nothing in his face gave him away, but the quick gleam of something like admiration in his eyes told her she'd hit on the truth. He continued to smile at her with that half smile that mocked and taunted and said, "Are you going to ask me out for dinner?"

"I can't imagine why I should."

"Then your imagination is less wide-ranging than I thought it was from reading your column."

She sighed. "Mr. Garrett, I want you to know that I've . . . I want . . ." She turned slightly to face him, bracing herself to take the full brunt of those gleaming blue eyes head on. "Let's

33

call a truce, shall we? I won't be writing about you in any future columns, I can promise you that."

"Calling down the colors so soon? And all because of my request for an invitation to dinner." He lifted a hand and ran a slow, deliberate finger down her cheek. His touch mocked, insulted . . . burned. "Now you *are* beginning to interest me."

She flinched away from his hand. His eyes narrowed in speculation. "Clem told me you had a platonic arrangement with your stockbroker. Did he know what he was talking about?"

He *had* been busy. He had searched out her apartment, found the coffee shop she often frequented, and talked to Clem. Worst of all was the thought that Clem had given Garrett the answers he sought. An angry warmth flooded her cheeks. "Don't most people have platonic arrangements with their stockbrokers?"

Despite himself, he smiled. "But as I'm learning, you are not most people."

"My . . . relationship with my stockbroker is none of your business."

"You're not going to hide behind him and pretend he's your lover?"

"I don't have to hide behind anybody." She got up from the booth to leave.

He caught her arm. "Have dinner with me tonight."

"I'm sorry. I have another engagement." She twisted her wrist, trying to free herself from his hold. She didn't succeed.

"Break it."

The order came out flat and cool, as if he expected her immediate agreement. She stiffened her arm, resisting that slight tugging motion that pulled her toward him. The pads of his fingers pressed into the sensitive area of her pulse, and she had the feeling that he knew exactly how fast her heart was beating . . . and why. "Let go of me, please."

She hated the breathless quality of her voice and hoped he would attribute her shallow breathing to anger and not to the fact that he was touching her.

34

His eyes darkened. "You're very brave on paper, Ms. O'Neill. But meeting me face-to-face seems to be another story."

It certainly was another story, one she had no intention of writing. Behind him, Tom coughed. She lifted her eyes to find the older man leaning casually on the counter, watching the two of them with an interested grin. Her cheeks went fiery. "You're making a scene." Garrett glanced up at Tom, heeded her appeal, and released her.

Filled with relief, she lifted her head and looked him squarely in the eye. "Good-bye, Mr. Garrett. Rest easy in your bed tonight. You're safe from any further probings from my pen. I will also make sure that we don't 'accidentally' bump into each other."

His anger had subsided. His lazy smile sent a chill from the nape of her neck to the base of her spine. The gleam in his eyes trapped her more surely than his hand on her wrist had. She felt as if she couldn't move or breathe. "Is that thought supposed to make me rest easy in my bed?"

"It should."

"It doesn't." His lips lifted in a smile.

"There simply is no pleasing you, is there, Mr. Garrett?"

His eyes gleamed. "There might be. Care to try?"

No longer able to take his lazy baiting, knowing it was the way he treated any woman he believed to be throwing herself at him, she whirled around and ran up the steps of the coffee shop, knowing full well she had been routed.

"Score one to the enemy," she said under her breath and knew she would never see him again. The thought should have cheered her. It didn't.

Her only thought when she returned to her apartment was to give Clem C. Davis a piece of her mind. She dialed his number with shaking fingers.

Helen's soft voice answered. "Oh, hello, Rana. It's good to hear from you. I suppose you're calling in reply to my invitation."

"Invitation?" Rana paused, momentarily distracted. She recognized those soothing tones. Getting a telephone call from someone who was mad as fire at Clem was no new experience for Helen. Clem's wife was extremely proficient in drawing the aggressor into conversation and defusing the anger aimed at her husband.

Helen went on cheerfully, "You haven't received your mail yet? Well, no matter. I'll issue your invitation over the phone. We're having an impromptu reception here tomorrow afternoon at three o'clock for Luc Garrett. Dinner will be at six. Clem and I both want you to come."

"I'm sorry, Helen. I . . . have other plans."

Helen was not easily put off. "I know it's short notice, but couldn't you cancel them? Luc is only going to be in town for a short time."

"I'm afraid not." She hated to turn Helen down. She was a good friend. If there was a dishonest or malicious bone in her body, Rana hadn't found it. Any woman who lived with Clem for thirty-five years and still maintained a cheerful sanity qualified for sainthood, and in Rana's opinion, Helen did. Helen had been nothing but gracious to Rana over the years. There was a time when Rana spent many hours with Clem. He had even dragged her home with him to stay for a week once when she'd been evicted from her apartment because she couldn't pay the rent. Another less confident woman might have questioned Clem's affection for Rana and treated her spitefully, but Helen never had. Rana considered Helen as good a friend as Clem . . . except that, at the moment, she wasn't sure Clem was her friend.

Rana asked to speak to Clem. No, he wasn't home, Helen told her. Should she have him call Rana when he came home? Rana told her yes, that she needed to talk to him quite urgently. Helen told her she would, and if Rana had been a more suspicious woman, she would have thought there was a hint of laughter in Helen's voice. Helen let a beat of time go by and then said, "Lucas asked specifically that you come tomorrow, Rana. He'll be very disappointed if you don't."

"I doubt that."

"Do you?" Helen's voice had that knowing sound. "I think it might be prudent for you to come."

"Prudent?"

Another silence, as if Helen was thinking over her next words. "Lucas isn't the type of man who is easily thwarted."

Helen was honest with her; she deserved to know the truth. "Helen, whatever you're thinking . . . it isn't true. We met this morning at a . . . coffee shop. We talked. I . . . promised him I wouldn't . . . wouldn't bother him again. I intend to keep that promise." She played with the telephone cord, wrapping it around her finger. "So you see . . . whatever he said earlier in the week . . . no longer applies."

"I see." Helen sounded thoughtful. "Is that the message I should relay to him?"

"No! No. Just say that I had other plans that I couldn't cancel."

Helen's agreement was grudging. After thanking her for the invitation, Rana hung up the phone, refusing to ponder on the reason Lucas Garrett had requested her presence at Helen's party.

She worked on her column that morning, trying to get some ideas for Monday. Nothing earthshaking occurred. She'd have to work on it tomorrow. She was committed to cooking a meal for that night, and she knew she had to start in the middle of the day in order to assure that everything was ready. She prepared the food, doing the things ahead that she could. She had planned to fix Philip an Oriental meal of lemon chicken dipped in rice flour served with the sweet-tart lemon sauce that took hours of stirring. Mushrooms, bean sprouts, and water chestnuts served as the combined vegetable and salad, and for dessert she made tiny sugar cookies sprinkled with red and green and yellow-colored sugar that looked like so many Christmas baubles lying on the counter. The meal took all afternoon, and when it was almost seven, she realized she had to fly to get ready. Feeling grubby and hot, knowing she had flour on her

37

nose, she went to jump into the shower, when the doorbell rang. She muttered a curse under her breath. It wasn't Philip, it couldn't be. Phil was far too punctilious to arrive this far ahead of time.

From outside her door, in the hallway of the apartment, the youthful male voice that had just changed yelled, "Hey, Brooke Shields. Open up."

She tied the robe around her tighter and released the chain lock. Outside stood a teenager in faded jeans and his favorite purple shirt. At sixteen, Terry Clark hovered on the brink of manhood with a grudging good-will and ambiguity about growing up that Rana remembered from her own youth. "Well, if it isn't E.T. What's the matter? Did you miss the last saucer home?"

"Get smart with me, Brooke, and I'll hide your makeup case."

"That won't make a bit of difference to me. What do you want, Terry?"

"Mom wants to know if she can borrow some sesame seeds." Terry, who was just on the verge of becoming a very attractive young man, thrust a hand through his mop of rusty brown hair, yanked down his T-shirt in vivid purple that said Rush, and grinned at her.

"Is she going to bring them back again?" Rana asked dryly.

Terry looked up at the ceiling as if considering it. He knew she was correcting his usage of the word just as she had done many times before. It never seemed to have the slightest effect on him. "I don't think so. She's making homemade bread sticks. I might snitch a couple and give you one."

"Thanks, pal. You're all heart."

"Wanna arm wrestle?" Terry followed her into the kitchen and leaned against the doorway to watch while she opened the cupboard door and brought out the requested seeds.

"I can't right now. I don't have time."

"You got company coming for dinner?"

"Yes."

38

He raised an eyebrow and looked like a comic wise owl. "Some guy?"

"Are you writing a gossip column?"

"You don't usually have guys come here."

"Have you been counting?"

Terry rubbed his nose and moved his sneakered feet, adjusting his spine into a more comfortable position against the door. "I just never thought you were that gone on guys."

"Well, there's degrees of 'gone.'"

Terry thought about that. "Mom's been reading your column. She says you're giving some guy hell."

"Watch your talk, E.T., or I'll ship you off on the next Klingon spaceship."

He looked around, casting his eyes casually over the cookies, his nose sniffing the air appreciatively. Suddenly he thrust his arm out and pointed behind her back. "Look over there. Something's burning!"

She faced him, her eyes knowing. "That trick went out with Robin Hood. If you want a cookie, ask for one."

"Like a kid, you mean?" He wrinkled his nose. "That's no fun. I'd rather cop one." But he reached for a cookie anyway, and she smiled when he gathered up two. He put one in his mouth and chewed reflectively. "Pretty good, O'Neill," he said around the cookie.

"Thanks, Clark."

"You're welcome. Got any milk?"

"Anything else you'd like? Dancing girls?" She poured a glass out and handed it to him. Terry accepted it, his eyes on her as he tipped the glass to his mouth. "I don't know. Are they cute?"

She shook her head in exasperation. He said, "What have you got against this guy, anyway?"

"Did you read the column?"

He drank his milk, lowered the glass, and squinted at her. "Read something? What would I want to do that for?" It was a running battle between them. Rana chided him for spending too

39

much time with the video games; he called her a "disk" jockey because her word processor used software disks and threatened to buy her a holster for her dictionary because she was always losing it. Terry did well in school, but it was his quick intelligence that kept his grades respectable, not his diligence.

"Well, if you had, you would know what I've got against him, wouldn't you?"

"You mean you're not gonna tell me?"

"You want to find out something in this world, kid, you gotta do it yourself."

"Yeah, but reading, that's a pretty drastic step to take."

She shrugged and held out the cup full of seeds. "That's the price you pay for curiosity."

She cast an anxious look at the clock and gestured toward the door. "Come on, Clark, clear out. I've got to get ready."

"I'm not sure I want to go just yet. Maybe I'll stick around and say hi to the stockbroker. He's always good for a laugh—"

"Out!" She turned him around and began to push him down the entryway. He gave her just enough resistance to show her he was allowing her to push him around. At sixteen, he was more than a match for her in size and weight, and if he had really wanted to stay, she would never have been able to budge him. "You're getting scrawny, O'Neill," he said over his shoulder.

"You're getting mouthy, Clark. Now get out of here." In spite of his halfhearted resistance, she pushed him through her apartment door. He turned. "Give me the handshake, Rana." She obliged, grasping him at thumb, wrist, hand, and elbow, finishing with the ritual dusting of palms. She smiled at his grinning face. "And don't spill the sesame seeds in the hall." She turned him around and began to push him toward the elevator.

A man stood in the hallway by her door. He took in the entire scene with sharp blue eyes, his gaze moving over her hands on Terry's back, her robe, her disheveled hair, her bare face. She stopped pushing Terry so abruptly that he fell back

40

against her and squeezed her between the wall and his young, muscular body, knocking the breath out of her.

"Jeez, I'm sorry, Rana." He leaped away and turned to put his hands on her shoulders. "Are you okay?"

"If she is," Lucas Garrett's cool voice said, "it's no thanks to you."

Terry faced her, his back to Garrett, and said in a low tone, "Some dinner guest. I thought the stockbroker was coming. This dude looks like he just rode in off the range and hitched his horse to a parking meter. Not your usual style. But he looks a lot more with it than that other creep." Terry's hand came up and his fingers flicked over her face. "Sorry I kept you from getting ready for him. You've still got flour on your nose." He twisted around and gave Lucas Garrett a sketchy salute and a grin. "Have a good night." He accented the last two words with a puckish humor that made Rana want to kick him. Then he disappeared into the elevator, turning around to raise his arm and flop his hand to them in a silly kid's wave as the doors closed.

"Wiseacre kid," Lucas Garrett said, his eyes on her. "Friend of yours?"

"Sometimes I'm not sure." She hesitated, unsure of what to do, still breathless from the knock against the wall Terry had given her.

He looked at her, a strange expression in his eyes, and said, "Are you all right?"

"I think so, although I won't really know for another ten minutes until my body stops reverberating." She pushed herself away from the wall. "That kid must weigh more than I thought he did."

Garrett drawled, "Somehow I don't see you as the motherly type."

"Neither does Terry," she said, her voice clipped, her chin coming up. "I'm a combination sister and surrogate father to him."

"Father?" One dark brown eyebrow arched in mockery.

41

"I provide an outlet for his need to indulge in horseplay with an adult."

"I see." There was a new light in his eyes, one she didn't particularly care for. "May I come in?"

"I . . . it's a bit inconvenient at the moment."

He didn't move. "I won't stay long."

"If you stay five seconds, it will be too long, Mr. Garrett. I'm expecting a dinner guest, and I have to shower and change—"

The gleam in his eyes brightened. "I won't stop you."

"Whatever you have to say to me can be said—"

"No . . . not in the hallway." He took her arm and pushed her into the entryway ahead of him and closed the door behind him. He wasn't wearing a jacket and the sleeves of his shirt brushed her arm. She drew back involuntarily. "I . . ."

As he looked around the room, his fingers tightened on her wrist. She could see his mind working, almost taking inventory, not of the things that were there, but the things that weren't. He saw the lack of family photographs, the barren walls, the single color scheme brightened only by the huge pillows for sitting that were scattered on the pale rug.

"Interesting. Where will your dinner guest sit? Or do you just go immediately to the bedroom?"

She swallowed hard, choking back angry words. "What was it you wanted to see me about?"

He walked away from her and went to the window. "Nice view."

"Mr. Garrett," she said through clenched teeth. "I realize I haven't endeared myself to you, but I think this form of revenge is rather childish. I have a dinner guest, I need a shower, I'm in a hurry. Would you please just say whatever it is you have to say and leave?"

She stared at his back, wondering if that was tension she saw in the broad shoulders. He stood looking out her window for a moment longer and then he turned, his eyes finding hers, his blue eyes guarded. "But there you're wrong, Ms. O'Neill."

"Where?" she said foolishly.

"You have"— there was a pause, and the blue eyes gleamed —"endeared yourself to me."

She said impatiently, "That's ridiculous."

"So much so that I was destroyed by your refusal to come to Helen and Clem's tomorrow."

She stared at him owlishly. "I didn't know you did stand-up comedy routines."

His eyes moved over her face, and she wondered if she still had flour on her nose. There was something distinctly strange about his perusal. She had the feeling he was holding back amusement.

He said, "My audience isn't laughing."

"No, of course I'm not laughing. The whole thing is too ludicrous to be believed." She took a breath. "Let's be honest with each other, Mr. Garrett."

"I thought we were," he murmured before she could finish her thought.

She glared at him. "You're annoyed and angry, and you've come to annoy and anger me. Well, you've succeeded. You may ride away from my door, knowing that you have been successful in making me wish I had never seen you on television and decided to write about you. . . ."

His eyes flared with a sudden, understanding gleam that made her heart sink. She watched that kindling flame begin to burn. Knowing she had started the conflagration, she kept her chin high. He took a step toward her. "So it wasn't my books that aroused your interest," he said, in a cool, low tone. "It was my appearance."

"You flatter yourself."

"But as you said in your column, I can hardly help it, can I? That's the way women look at me."

"At least you've got that part right."

"Oh, I do know how to read and retain information." He watched her, giving her the feeling she was a mouse in a trap that was about to close. "I also know something about a writer's motivation." He took a step closer.

43

She fought the wild urge to step back. "Motivation?"

There was no question about it. He was stalking her. He advanced another step, and her breathing began to quicken. She could feel the blood coursing in her veins, her heart thumping. She wanted desperately to turn and run from the apartment. Those well-shaped lips looked far too skilled, too generous, too warm. "Emotion," she said, her voice husky. "Emotion motivates a writer."

"That's right," he agreed, his words heavy with satisfaction. "Writers write out of deep feeling. Wild, untamed feeling, the primitive urge to create . . ." He took hold of the belt of her robe and used it to tug her forward.

Her body burned. "Don't," she whispered, but instead of warning, there was hesitancy, curiosity . . . and anticipation in the husky word, and he knew it.

His head lowered and his tongue came out and touched her cheek.

She pulled away from him as if he had touched her with a searing iron.

"It's sugar." He sounded surprised. "I haven't tasted red candy sugar since I was a kid." His lips moved over her face, his tongue exploring, teasing.

"Don't—"

"Don't what?" He kissed her nose, her eyelashes.

"Don't do this." His warm mouth moved over her cheek like a drift of summer breeze. "I don't want—"

"You do want," he murmured. "You want as much as I want." He took her mouth with an eager hungriness that aroused an answering fire deep within her. The raw burst of emotion inside her was unexpected . . . and powerful. His hands on her back felt so right, so good. The warmth of his body heated hers through the robe while his mouth took possession, asking and answering questions that had no words.

He was right. She did want. She wanted so much.

He lifted his head and looked down into her face, his eyes gleaming with his new knowledge of her in them. There was no mockery there, only the delight of discovery. His hands moved over her back, finding a more intimate curve of her hips and cupping his palm over the rounded bones just below her waist. She could feel the separate, individual weight of each one of his fingers. "I'll be here to pick you up at five o'clock tomorrow afternoon."

"No—" Her protest was automatic.

"If you aren't here," he murmured in her ear, "I'll know it's because you're a coward."

"I'm not a coward."

"But you issue challenges you don't intend to follow up on."

Her eyes flashed up at him. "I didn't issue you a challenge . . ." She pushed at him.

He stood unmoving, still holding her. "Oh, yes, you did, honey. I got the message loud and clear . . . and so did most of the population of New York."

He stood looking at her for a moment, his hands clasped on her hips, his eyes dark and amused. She braced herself against him, her hands around his upper arms. Under the crisp oxford cloth she felt the hard muscles.

"If you don't come with me," he said softly, "you'll generate more fuel for the fire."

"What . . . do you mean?"

"Use your head, O'Neill. Half of the people at Clem's house tomorrow work on a newspaper somewhere. The other half are in television or filmmaking. If we show up together—some of the speculation about us will die down."

His fingers slid away from her waist, but he didn't step away. He couldn't. She was holding him too tightly.

"At least," he said softly, neither looking down at the tight fingers that held him . . . nor moving away from her, "it should . . . unless we give them something new to think about."

She relaxed at once and pulled her hands away from him.

"Five o'clock," he said, watching her.

"No," she said.

He smiled, and only when he nodded and went out the door did she realize that her "no" had been far too soft and tentative to be taken seriously.

CHAPTER THREE

"I don't think I quite have your undivided attention."

Phil had been talking about the stock market, and she'd been trying to listen, trying to keep her eyes fastened on him. He half-lay across from her in the Roman arrangement she'd made for dining, pillows stacked all around for reclining in a cozy nest, a white cloth spread on the floor between them. They had finished eating only moments ago, and he had assured her everything was delicious. Now she sat with her legs crossed, her head bent, her eyes on the glimmering white liquid in her glass. She was glad Phil had enjoyed the meal. She couldn't remember eating a thing.

"I'm listening." She raised her eyes to him. He looked at her quizzically, his own wineglass held idly in his long, thin fingers as he reclined against a bright purple pillow. He'd taken off his jacket before they started to eat, but he still wore his tie, correctly caught with a clasp. Somehow, lounging as he was against the pillows like an Arabian sheik in his custom-fit shirt and Brooks Brothers suit pants, he looked faintly ludicrous, like an adult trying to play a child's game.

She lifted her wine to take a sip. When she lowered the glass, Phil shook his head and said, "No, I don't think you were listening. You seem . . . distracted. Your column going badly?"

She shook her head. As she turned to set the glass on the tray, the silky yellow sleeve of the jump suit she wore fell away from her arm. At the sight of her pale flesh, a strange gleam sprang to life in Phil's eyes. It was a sensual gaze, a look a man gives a woman. Disconcerted, thinking only of distracting him, she said suddenly, "I was thinking about courage." She rubbed her hand over the corner of the velvet pillow she lay on.

Phil stared at her, plainly thrown off guard. "Courage?" He held the glass suspended in midair in front of him, waiting for her answer.

"I was wondering if I have it."

There was a strange little moment of silence. Then Phil tipped his head to drink the rest of his wine, put the glass down on the black-lacquered tray in the middle of the tablecloth, and leaned back against the cushions again. The look he gave her made her think he might have misinterpreted her remark to mean something much more . . . personal. Dear God. Did he think she was trying to tell him in an oblique way that she was ready to make love with him?

"Of course you do. You write a syndicated column for a living." He smiled at her. "That takes fortitude."

His words were innocuous, but Rana's nerves prickled. Was he probing cautiously? She stared beyond him, her mind filled suddenly with the dark face of a man who didn't probe cautiously, who was as direct and forceful as a western wind. "Does it?" She moved suddenly, gathering her feet under her to collect the dishes from their meal. She piled the plates onto the tray, thinking that she didn't like herself very much right at the moment. She was entertaining one man . . . and thinking about another.

She lifted the tray and escaped toward the kitchen, leaving Phil lying there, that quizzical look in his eyes, a half smile lifting his mouth.

She couldn't remember a time when she'd ever actually shared her thoughts with Phil. He was accustomed to light conversation, easy talk, talk that filled the silences but never went below the surface. He never said anything about his personal feelings, and neither did she. Their relationship depended on his critiques of a ballet performance, their discussion of a concert, or Phil's precise dissection of a play. For all his pragmatism in matters of money, Phil was a frustrated drama critic, and he could spend hours discussing how the female lead had botched her timing and fallen out of character in the second act, how the set hadn't really worked, and how the director must have gone to school for early medieval history instead of drama.

But she wasn't the only one who had broken the rules. He had never looked at her like that before.

She set the tray down on the sink . . . and nearly jumped out of her skin when she felt his hands on her shoulders.

"What kind of courage were you looking for?"

She hadn't been imagining his thoughts after all. She turned, trying to wrench his hands off her shoulders. He merely shifted his grip, allowing her to face him. She said, "Not . . . what you're thinking."

He seemed not to hear her. "Rana . . ." He drew her closer, his face soft.

His hands on her shoulders and the look in his eyes put her in a mild state of panic. She didn't want this. He leaned down, his mouth inches away from hers.

She said, "Would you . . . care for some more wine?"

"No, I don't want wine." His hands moved down to the small of her back, and she resisted, her hands on his chest pushing him away.

"Are you playing games with me?" he asked.

"If I am, I'm not doing it very well."

The rueful honesty in her tone made him pause. "Rana, listen to me. I know you were wary of me because of the divorce, but now—"

She twisted out of his arms, facing him. "I don't want a serious relationship with you or any other man."

Impatience flitted over his darkly controlled face. "Sometimes I think you aren't really a woman."

She stiffened in pride and pain. "I think you'd better go."

His hands dropped to his sides. "What was all that talk about courage?"

"It had nothing to do with you."

"I don't think very much in your life does have to do with me."

"We're friends, the way we both wanted to be friends. . . ."

He shook his head. "Friendship was your idea, not mine. I was willing to wait until you were ready. Now I see you never will be."

She stood staring up at him for a long moment, feeling the pang of loss. Then she turned away, her brown head glossy in the light. "I'll get your coat."

His silence was agreement. She left him standing in her kitchen and went in to retrieve his jacket from the cushion on the floor. But when she rose, he was there behind her. She handed it to him, and he took it easily, his face once again smooth with blandness. At the door he said, "I was wrong. You are a coward, Rana." He turned and went out the door, shutting it softly behind him.

She spent a restless night. She knew that everything that Phil had said was true. She was a coward. Facing Lucas Garrett and going with him to Clem and Helen's house wouldn't prove a thing. Her bravery was already suspect. And so, with all the logical, careful arguments in her mind marshaled, her hand ready to pick up the phone and tell Garrett she wasn't going with him, on Sunday afternoon she dressed carefully and was ready long before the doorbell rang.

"Hello," he said, looking down at her, making the word seem more than it was.

"Come in." She needed something to do with her hands. "Can I get you something to drink?" He was just as devastating in the standard business attire for males on the Eastern seaboard as he was in western clothes. Dressed in a summer blazer the color of buttermilk, a crisp shirt that was probably custom-made to fit his broad shoulders and narrow waist, a suitable and correct brown silk tie, and moroccan shoes under his brown pants that were made of soft, expensive wool, he looked like a successful executive rather than a renegade writer.

"I'll wait and have something at Clem's."

"Fine." She moved to collect her purse, anxious to be out of the apartment. Garrett, on the other hand, seemed inclined to linger. He relaxed back against the corner of the entryway wall. "Monochrome," he said, his eyes moving over the brown silk dress she wore that matched her hair and was just one shade darker than her tanned skin. "Interesting. A silky brown cat with gray eyes."

"Is that a compliment?"

"I think perhaps I'm warning myself to remember the claws before I stroke the pretty fur. Are you tan like that all over?"

This time she'd prepared herself. She wasn't going to give him the satisfaction of disconcerting her. "Research, Mr. Garrett?"

He shook his head slowly. "Uh, uh. If it were research, I wouldn't ask, I'd investigate."

She picked up her leather kidskin purse from one of the rug-covered cubes and, anxious to increase the distance between them, opened the apartment door. "I keep having to remind myself that you make your living saying outrageous things."

"Ah, but then"—he followed her out and closed the door behind her—"so do you, Rana O'Neill."

A few minutes later, seated in the backseat of a taxi, they rode together in a silence that was broken only by the usual blare of horns in the streets. It wasn't an angry silence; it was, surprisingly enough, a comfortable one. Clem lived out on Long Island, in the high-rent district on the Sound. The old house had been in his family for generations. If it hadn't, Clem would never have been able to afford it. But they did have a long ride ahead of them. She settled back against the corner of the seat, trying not to be quite so aware of the strength and closeness of Lucas Garrett's thigh inches away from hers on the seat.

The taxi driver aimed himself at their destination like a guided missile with a charmed existence. Though the Sunday afternoon traffic in the heated city was light, he drove like a demon escaping hell. Nothing stopped him. He wedged the car

51

between a truck and the curb on a one-way street, and Garrett grimaced.

"Something wrong?"

"If that idiot sends me to that Last Big Round up in the Sky, you will inform my next of kin, won't you?"

She laughed. "I'll certainly try."

Garrett said, looking at her, "Clem tells me you worked for him during the years he put the *Indiana News* on the map."

"Yes." She looked away from those straightforward blue eyes, gazing out the window, where she saw nothing.

"You must have gone with him about the time your parents were separated."

She kept her face cool and smooth. "Yes, I did." She didn't ask how he had known about her parents. Everyone in the world knew about her parents.

"You must have been about eighteen then."

"Actually," she said with no emotion at all, "I was one hundred and two."

There was a silence as he digested that. Not wanting his sympathy and relieved when he didn't express any, she said politely, "What about you?" The taxi lurched around a corner. She grabbed an armrest and said, "Where are those next of kin you want me to inform of your demise in case it should happen?"

He smiled, a warm, wonderful smile. "My parents are still on the ranch near Ten Sleep . . . along with a brother, a sister, her husband, and their two children."

"So all that publicity hype is true?"

He gave a wry look. "Depends on what publicity hype you're talking about."

"The all-American boy brought up straight as an arrow in the best western tradition."

He twisted in the seat and smiled at her, a strange, half-mocking smile. "I suppose essentially that's correct. What about you? Weren't you brought up as the all-American girl?"

"Not exactly. Although I didn't know it at the time. I was

blissfully unaware that the rest of the world didn't live like we did. I thought all little girls had a special suitcase for their security blankets and went to sleep at night in motels to the beat of a typewriter."

"My ex-wife used to complain about that."

She searched her mind, trying to remember what she had read about him. She'd never heard that he had been married. For as long as she could remember, he'd been on all the most eligible bachelor lists. He must have married very young, in his twenties, perhaps. He couldn't be more than thirty-five or thirty-six now.

"I used to put my head under the pillow. How did your wife solve the problem?"

Luc looked at her. "By divorcing me."

"Drastic, but effective," she murmured.

He let her outrageous comment echo in the silence of the car . . . until the taxi swerved to dash into an empty space in the left-hand lane. He grabbed the armrest on his side. "I'm glad you're not afraid," he said. "I'm terrified."

He wasn't really, but he was apprehensive, and he was man enough not to hide it or be ashamed of it. She laughed, admiring him in spite of herself. "Would you believe that cab drivers really have very few accidents?"

"No. But tell me that anyway. I need all the consolation I can get. Maybe even"—his eyes flickered over her—"a strong woman to hold my hand."

With his face carefully held in an expression of mock innocence in what was undoubtedly Lucas Garrett's idea of quaking fear, he held his hand out, palm out. She smiled at him, laughter in her eyes, but made no move to place her hand in his.

He didn't take it away as she thought he would, and the mock innocence disappeared to be replaced by a male challenge, a cool asking that was more subtle—and more dangerous.

In the taxicab the atmosphere changed. His eyes dared, mocked, compelled her. Staring at him, her arm moved upward.

His long, blunt-ended fingers closed over hers instantly. Warm, masculine . . . and very good to touch, his hand radiated security . . . and strength.

"I don't deserve this," she said huskily.

"What don't you deserve?" The face he turned to her was cool and bland.

"Your . . . being kind to me."

"What makes you think I'm being kind to you?"

"Aren't you?"

"I wouldn't call it that."

A chill touched her. "Are you seeking vengeance?"

He gave her a mocking look. "Not vengeance. My goal is vindication . . . among other things," he said, that smile playing over his face.

Her reaction was involuntary and immediate. She tugged at her hand, but he was too quick for her. His fingers tightened. She was caught.

"If you think you're going to convince me to tell my readers what a terribly nice man you are, you're mistaken."

He looked at her, his blue eyes clear and cool. "I don't give a damn what you tell your readers."

"What do you give a damn about, Mr. Garrett?"

"A woman who calls me 'Mr. Garrett' in a stiff little voice." He wasn't smiling.

"Let go of my hand." Her voice was low and angry. The cabbie couldn't have heard exactly what she said, but he must have heard the agitated tone. He glanced into the rearview mirror, as if checking to see if he had an argument developing in the backseat that bore watching.

"I don't think so, Ms. O'Neill." The accent on her title was silky and faintly menacing. "From now on, it's no holds barred." He turned her hand over and captured her fingers between his palm and his thigh.

The shock of that hard-muscled leg under her hand jolted her . . . but Garrett wasn't finished. He began to move his hand gently over hers, tracing the tendons that led to her fingers. Her face hot, her entire body aware of the hard man's thigh beneath her fingers and the gentle stroking over their tops, she sat rigid and immobile, telling herself she was a fool to have dropped her guard with him for even a minute. He was playing a game with her, trying to make her think he was interested in her as a woman. She wouldn't fall for that, not for a minute.

"I think you've forgotten the purpose of this little outing."

"Have I?"

"We were going to confound everyone with our amiability toward each other."

"You mean I'm supposed to pretend I like you?" she asked in a dry tone that brought the beginning of a smile to his mouth.

"Too tough an assignment?"

"Much too tough. Far beyond my acting ability."

"Too bad." He didn't sound worried. His fingers drifted over the bones of her hand, stopping to make light circles over her knuckles. She had been touched by men before, and last night Phil had held her, but she had never felt anything like the leap of nerves under the light pressure of those fingers that were massaging her skin over her bones in an erotic caress. Slowly, carefully, almost as if she weren't aware of what she was doing, she eased her hand away.

She was filled with relief—until she looked up into his face. Luc Garrett was smiling an attractive, soul-destroying smile.

She looked away, her pulse leaping in her throat. She'd been a fool to come out with him. What was she trying to prove?

After a small eternity, they reached the house. She felt stiff and awkward getting out of the car in front of Luc. Tension had made her muscles taut. She was wound up tight, and all Luc Garrett had done was touch her hand.

She went up the steps, her head high. Luc Garrett was the last man in the world she could ever get involved with. She knew that, even if he didn't. What were his motives? What was he trying to do to her? It was a subtle warfare, she knew that, but the trouble was, she didn't know what he wanted. Was it her pride? A retraction in her column? It certainly couldn't have been the more obvious thing. She had attacked him on his most vulnerable front, his writing. He couldn't be interested in her sexually. It just wasn't possible.

A quarter of a mile in the distance, the wash of the Atlantic Ocean tumbled relentlessly. He'd have to wait until that ocean stopped rolling if that was what he wanted. She could never get involved with Luc Garrett. He was a writer.

A heat haze hung in the air, but as she climbed the steps to the airy veranda that ran around the entire house, the breeze from the Sound flattened the brown silk dress against her body and swirled the skirt around her nylon-clad thighs. Garrett was a step or two behind her and he made a small sound but she had no idea what the sound meant and she didn't want to speculate on the possibilities. He was too smooth, too calculating. She wouldn't fall under his spell, she couldn't.

Inside the house Helen descended on them, beaming, her short, slight figure stunning in draped blue silk. "Rana. Lucas." Her small arms circled Garrett's waist, and he bent to enable her to press a kiss on his cheek. "It's good to see you. What can I get you to drink?"

"Perrier water for me," Lucas Garrett said easily.

Rana's eyes flashed with surprise. "I'll have a gin and tonic."

When Helen bustled away, Rana said in a low tone, "Not drinking today, Mr. Garrett?"

He gave her a cool, sweeping look that raised the temperature of the room by several degrees. "I always like to keep a clear head when I engage the enemy in action."

Deliberately, she turned away from Luc, seeking out Clem with her eyes. He was standing in a group with three other men, holding court, gesturing with his drink. "Do you consider Clem your enemy?"

Her gray eyes swung back to Luc, knowing the answer, defying him to say it.

"No," he said, carefully, watching her, "you are the enemy."

He watched as her eyes darkened. This was a dangerous game, and he knew it. She played the part of a successful career woman well, but under that facade resided a complex and sensitive woman. A woman with courage. Any other woman would have walked away from him after he openly declared her the enemy, but Rana hadn't.

How bleak she'd sounded in the cab when they had touched on the subject of her mother and father. Her parents had had a stormy marriage that ended in tragedy. Was Rana carrying scars? She'd have to be very insensitive if she wasn't. And he knew she wasn't insensitive.

She stood her ground and met his eyes steadily. "I'm not your enemy, Mr. Garrett."

"Here we are." It was Helen again, at her smiling hostess best, carrying their drinks in her hand. "You two must circulate and meet the rest of our guests."

Rana knew Helen didn't contrive to separate them. She plainly expected Rana to follow Luc's trail around the room. But Rana drifted away on the pretense of speaking to an old friend.

Luc felt Rana go, felt the absence of her behind him like a sharp pang. He wanted to grind his teeth in frustration, but there was nothing he could do. Helen was a skillful hostess, and Luc was obliged to move around the room and speak to people, since Helen had organized the afternoon for the sole purpose of introducing him to the brighter lights in the newspaper world. Some of them he knew from the old *Indiana News* days, and in renewing an acquaintance with Al Henshaw, the editor of the opinion and editorial columns, he discovered that he had missed meeting Rana by a few short days. Restless, distracted, he had left in April of that year to try writing a novel and see how well he could survive on a semistarvation diet. Rana had joined the staff shortly after that.

But no matter where he was in the room, no matter who he was talking to, he was conscious of Rana. Once, when Henshaw stopped to take a breath in his long narrative, Luc lifted his glass to his lips. When he lowered it, he saw her across the room, her back to the window, her slim body in the brown silk

57

leaning against the frame, her long fingers wrapped around her glass. He recognized that determinedly interested look, for he had seen her wearing that look once before. She'd been out with her stockbroker then, sitting at a table in Tavern-on-the-Green. Was she deeply involved with the man? He hadn't thought so at the time. There was something about the way she walked out of the restaurant with him. Luc had learned to watch people to analyze the millions of little signals that they gave out to those they were with. He could read body language and knew how it showed what relationships people had with each other. Walking out of the restaurant that night, Rana O'Neill hadn't moved close to the man the way a woman would her lover. She hadn't smiled up at him or touched him or taken his arm.

Yet how well did he know her? Rana O'Neill was a bundle of contradictions. She kept pushing him away. And yet when he touched her, he had the most powerful urge to keep touching her. He wanted to touch her now. . . .

She could feel his eyes on her even though there were a dozen people standing about in Clem's living room. The late afternoon sunlight slanted through the wide room with its five windows open to their view of the sea, but Helen believed in keeping her house illuminated and her beloved chandelier was on, throwing out sparks of light that gleamed in the thick brown strands of Luc's hair. But the gleam of his hair was nothing compared to the dark glitter in his eyes.

She clutched her glass and turned away.

Two hours later she watched the chandelier's light shine on Al Henshaw's shiny pate as they sat around the table. They had nearly finished the main course of the meal. She felt full, warm and comfortable, sated with good food and good conversation and the gentle touch of the sea breeze that moved the filmy curtains at the bay window.

The seating arrangement had pleased her. Luc was as far away from her as possible, seated at the other end of the table. From the few discreet glances she'd managed in his direction, he seemed engaged in a politely urbane conversation with Beryl Diamond, the grande dame of the New York newspaper world. Clem, at the head of the table and her immediate right, had ignored Rana with the amiability of long acquaintance and talked across her nonstop, his voice rising as he expounded on the idiotic policies of the Administration to Henshaw, who sat on her other side and listened with a tolerant patience.

The discussion drifted to the new nominee for the vacant cabinet post of Health and Human Services. The nominee was a woman. From there the talk melted into women's rights. When all the old arguments had been quoted and requoted, Beryl, whom Rana knew had worked for three major papers during her lifetime, and who probably knew more about the hazards of breaking into a traditionally male work force than any other woman alive, said bluntly, "What good does talking or writing do—particularly if the talking or writing is done by women and aimed at men? Words don't change people's attitudes." She looked at Rana and said point-blank, "Do you think your column has changed Luc Garrett's mind about the kind of women characters he puts in his books?"

"Probably not," Rana answered easily, her eyes drifting to Luc, her lips curved in a smile.

He answered her with an equally lazy smile, as if he knew how much she enjoyed seeing him being thrust into the spotlight by Beryl Diamond's arrow-sharp tongue.

"You're right, Beryl," he said in that slow drawl, his eyes leaving Rana's. "Words don't change attitudes. But actions do. Now if Ms. O'Neill was really interested in influencing my ideas about women, she would agree to collaborate with me on my next book."

She sent him a sizzling look. He sat there and met the fire in her eyes, his face as beatific and innocent as Lucifer's. Wasn't there any way to disconcert that man?

Beryl's penciled eyebrows shot up, and her deep, manlike voice chortled. "Now there's a book I'd like to read."

The table was a long row of amused, interested faces turned

59

in her direction. The full import of what Luc had just done burst over her head like a thundercloud. He had just announced to representatives of three major New York newspapers and two television stations and a few assorted photographers that he wanted to collaborate on a book with her.

"Strange," Rana murmured, her voice growing soft as her temper soared. "I don't recall your asking me that, Mr. Garrett."

"Perhaps you were . . . distracted at the time." His voice implied the worst with such charm, and his smile hinted at dark, shared secrets.

You're an unscrupulous chauvinist, her eyes flashed to him across the room.

He read her meaning as accurately as if she had said it aloud. *Yes, but I'm a successful unscrupulous chauvinist.*

"Why don't you work on a book with Luc, Rana?" Helen said guilelessly. "You've always wanted to do fiction."

"No time. My column keeps me very busy. Luc will have to look for some other feminist to help him."

Beryl laughed and suggested Gloria Steinem and the conversation turned and Rana was eased out of the line of fire. She could have hugged Beryl.

But later, when they were sitting in the living room, Rana nestled comfortably into a corner of the couch a safe distance from Luc Garrett, her fingers clasping a tiny glass filled with apricot brandy, it was Beryl who brought up the subject again.

The older woman's majestic head turned to Luc. He sat on the stone hearth of the fireplace that was filled with flowers instead of a fire directly across from Rana, and he was drinking something dark and far more potent-looking than the sweet drink Rana had chosen. Yellow gladioli fanned out behind Luc's head. "What kind of a book were you thinking about writing with a female coauthor, Luc?"

"The same kind of book I always write," Luc said easily. "Otherwise it isn't a test."

"Maybe Rana would be more at home doing something contemporary."

"But I wouldn't," he said smoothly.

Rana asked, "Do you feel more confident conjuring up fictional events in the past, back in the days when men were men and women were women and everybody knew which was which?"

Luc eyed her, his smile easy. "There is something to be said for . . . a simpler time."

Without even thinking, Rana plunged. "A simpler time? Is that what you call it? A time when women had ten or twelve children and died at the age of thirty-five? A time when there was always a bedroom next to the kitchen because a woman was either taking care of a sick child or having another one?"

"All the more reason women needed the protection of a man."

"Those days are gone, thank God."

"Women still need to be protected from predatory men."

"That's true," she said softly. "Part of the problem is recognizing them."

"It isn't hard to recognize the one with his hand around your throat."

"Those kind I can handle."

"I don't believe you." He issued the soft male challenge into a room that suddenly became as still as a church.

Carefully, she reached out and put her glass on the table next to the couch and then sat up a little, her hands on her knees. "Try me."

His eyes glittered, and for a moment she thought he wasn't going to take up the gauntlet. Then, suddenly, without a word, he lunged at her.

She heard Beryl gasp, and then felt his hands on her shoulders dragging her down to Helen's white Persian rug. He lay half on top of her, his heavy weight pinning her to the floor. Rana's hand moved, and Luc Garrett moaned in pain and let go of her. In the next instant she was free and on her feet . . . and

61

Luc lay where she had rolled him to one side, his hand rubbing the nerve in his shoulder she had pinched with pinpoint accuracy.

Sounds of surprise filtered through the watching people. The men muttered words of sympathy for Luc; the women laughed nervously.

"Times have changed," Luc murmured, getting to his feet with an easy grace, his fingers still massaging the tender spot.

Rana faced him, watching, still wary. He might decide to come at her again in a desire to settle the score, and if he did, she would be ready.

Beryl let out a cackle of laughter. "I wish I had a camera to take a picture of the look on your face, Luc."

"I'm glad you don't." He sounded rueful, but not, somehow, embarrassed. His eyes found Rana's. "You're very good." He tipped his head in a sober little act of respect and then smiled at her, an action far more lethal to the beat of her heart than anything else he could have done. Why wasn't he angry? Why wasn't he trying to belittle her and regain his feeling of superiority? She'd wrestled him to the floor in front of his peers and friends. He should be furious. Instead, he said, "Care to share some of your expertise with me?"

His cool acceptance rocked her as his physical attack hadn't. He wasn't mocking her. He was serious.

She accepted his words in the spirit they were spoken . . . one writer asking another for information. "I'd be glad to. If you're free on a Saturday afternoon, you're welcome to come with me and visit the karate school I attend."

"I'll look forward to it," he murmured, that smile tilting the corner of his mouth.

With the male poise and lithe grace that were so much a part of him, Luc pulled at the knees of his trousers and lowered himself to the hearth again. Rana, in her slightly confused state, felt a weakness in her legs and an equal need to sit down. Helen bustled in and offered drinks and Beryl made an outrageous comment that Rana didn't catch but that had everyone laughing. Rana had the distinct feeling Beryl had made a joke at her expense, but there was nothing she could do about it nor did she want to. Luc's calm acceptance of the embarrassing episode and Beryl's humor made the awkward moment pass. Conversation flowed around her. She settled back, prepared to relax with the drink Helen had freshened for her when she looked up . . . to find Clem's eyes on her, raking her with a long, heavy-lidded, speculative look.

CHAPTER FOUR

In the taxi on the way home Luc sat quietly in the corner and looked out the window, his dark head turned away from her. He seemed immune to the driver's speedway techniques this time. No masculine hand sought hers when the car careened around a corner and dashed into an empty space in front of a truck. He was a million miles away, as remote as a star.

Rana turned away from him to watch as the glittering lights of New York slid by her window and wondered vaguely why she felt so bleak. He was reacting exactly as she knew he would. She had embarrassed and humiliated him, and though he took it well enough at the time, he was no longer interested in her.

She didn't want him to be interested in her. *Did she?*

When the taxi pulled up in front of her apartment building, Luc roused himself. "I'll walk you to the door," he said.

"It isn't necessary." She was out of the cab and coming round to his side.

"I know it isn't necessary," he said, that tone of amusement she was beginning to know filtering through his voice, "but humor me."

At the door he cupped her chin with warm fingers and caught her at the nape with his other hand. "I'm going to kiss you good night," he murmured in that same cool, amused tone, his mouth inches away from hers, "even though I may end up on the sidewalk."

His mouth moved closer to hers, his breath lightly brushing her lips. "Am I going to end up on the sidewalk, Rana?"

There was laughter and tenderness in his voice, a tenderness

65

that washed over her like a healing rain after his long silent ride beside her.

"Be brave, Garrett," she murmured back to him. "Try on some of that western courage you give the heroes in your books."

"Ah," he said, closing in a little more, his lips moving against hers as he talked to her, "but they don't run around trying to kiss women who can throw them two falls out of three."

Her hands came up under his jacket, finding the rounded smoothness of his muscles under the thin cloth of his shirt. He tensed, but she knew his tension wasn't from fear. He was feeling what she was feeling, a need, a stark, driving need. This was insanity, sheer insanity, sheer—his mouth settled with a sweet, hard warmth over hers, moving to fit the contours of hers—sheer heaven. She felt as if her bones were shifting to some new anatomical pattern that was better suited to fit the hard frame of Luc Garrett.

One of those lean-fingered hands drifted downward to slide silkily along her waist and down toward her hip and around to her bottom to lift her more intimately against him and fit her into the cradle of his hips. She felt it then, that first unfamiliar stirring of desire, low and deep.

She pulled back a little. He let her break off the kiss, but he held her just as closely as he had been.

She tipped her head back, looking at him with eyes gone brilliant in the darkness. "You're more than courageous. You're . . . lethal."

"No more than you." He bent to her again, taking her mouth more heatedly, pressing, flicking her lips lightly with his tongue. She responded, her body burning, her hips moving instinctively against him.

He murmured, "And here I was chastising myself all the way home because I thought I had turned you off totally, involving you in that show of strength."

"And I thought you were brooding about being bested."

He leaned away slightly to look down into her night-shadowed face and then, slowly, with what might have been reluctance, he released her. "When you know me better, Rana O'Neill, you'll understand that I'm not interested in winning or losing. I'm interested in that balance of power that happens between a man and a woman when they become lovers."

Before she could reply, he turned away. He climbed into the taxicab, leaving her to stand there and watch him go, the night breeze and the sound of the city the only things left behind . . . along with the sharp quivering feeling she couldn't repress.

Words. That was all they were. Words. He was an expert with words. But words could cut as well as thrill. Words could slice a woman into shreds. Words could kill a love, kill a marriage. . . . She unlocked her apartment and walked inside, knowing that her thoughts were all true and that she had to put Luc Garrett out of her mind . . . but still, his soft-spoken voice saying the words *when a man and woman become lovers* lingered in her ear.

Two nights later Lucas Garrett appeared alone on the television program she had been invited to share with him. She huddled under the covers, watching her television set from her bed. The moment he walked onto the set, Luc's extraordinary male grace and hard, lean face dominated the screen. He sat on the blue couch next to the interviewer, his long legs crossed, the tiny mike clipped to the edge of his stylishly narrow lapel. The program was videotaped, of course, but even so, Luc looked cool and male and infinitely attractive in living color. Those blue eyes of his photographed to perfection. Not only did he look good, he *was* good. He was smooth, articulate, and poised. He was also polite—but he steadfastly refused to talk about Rana.

After several unsuccessful tries to get Luc to open up on the subject of Rana, the interviewer said in that winningly boyish way that had endeared him to all of America, "Isn't it true that you and Rana O'Neill are feuding?"

No, Lucas told him, that was not true.

The carefully guileless questions continued. "But didn't she write a column about you saying that she didn't like the heroines in your books?"

Luc's smile lingered on that attractive mouth. "You'll have to ask her about that."

The man seated at the desk next to Luc smiled. It wasn't a smile of amusement. It was a self-satisfied, triumphant smile. Rana felt her blood cool and a chill shiver over her skin.

"I have here"—the TV star brought out a photo—"a picture of you and Miss O'Neill taken at a recent party."

Rana sat forward, her skin prickling. In that second or two it took for the camera to switch to a close-up of the photo, her heart accelerated. Where had they gotten a picture? Suddenly, there it was on the screen, a full-size shot of Luc lying on top of her, both of them flat on the floor. They had only been that way for an instant. Who had been quick-thinking enough to snap that picture? Her mind went back over the guest list. There had been two professional photographers there, both of them men. Either one of them was capable of a little subterfuge.

Whoever their nemesis was with the hidden camera, he was an expert. He had caught her expression well. Her face was tightly drawn in lines of surprise and anger.

"Would you care to explain this to the folks out there, Luc?"

The camera switched to Luc, and he looked just as smooth, just as calm as he had a moment ago. "I was helping Miss O'Neill demonstrate her karate routine."

"At a dinner party?" The host's eyebrows rose.

"We were talking about a woman's need for protection by a man." Luc paused, chuckled. "If you had taken a picture a few seconds later, you would have caught me writhing in pain on the floor. Miss O'Neill proved she could take care of herself quite adequately."

"Actually," the host said, in his cat-with-the-canary tone, "we do have a picture of you taken a few seconds later."

Again the wait. Again the photo. This one was of Luc on the floor, his face constricted, his hand on his shoulder . . . and Rana standing over him, her face flushed.

"Looks like that was one debate you lost, Luc." The audience laughed.

"Looks like," Luc said easily.

"Could it be that she's a better man than you are?"

"It could be," Luc said slowly, "that she's a better person than I am, smarter, more prepared to take care of herself."

The TV host sat back. "How do you, a writer of westerns, with macho men in them and the macho background and all that implies, how do you feel about being shown up by a woman half your size?"

"Actually," Luc leaned back against the couch and looked supremely relaxed, "I found being decked by Rana O'Neill a much pleasanter experience than being lanced in full view of half the country by you."

The audience burst into laughter and then applause, and the TV host laughed nervously but looked relieved to be announcing that it was time for a commercial break. While Rana sat there with hot cheeks, the phone rang.

She didn't answer it. She didn't move away from the television screen. When the commercial was over and the TV host returned, Luc Garrett was gone from the blue couch. In his place sat an actress.

The phone rang again. She ignored it and tossed the covers aside.

A half hour later she had showered and dressed and called Clem to find out where Luc was staying. To her surprise Clem told her Luc was staying in an elegant apartment house in a friend's condominium rather than a hotel.

She had a bit of difficulty talking the security guard into admitting her into the complex, but he had seen her picture in the paper, and he knew she was who she said she was. He had also seen the television program.

She walked into the open courtyard. Her face bathed in the warm summer heat of the night, she entered the building and took an elevator up to the fourth floor, where Clem had told her Luc was staying.

In front of the door, she hesitated. She wasn't altogether sure why she was here. She only knew she had to see Luc, had to tell him . . .

The door opened. He was wearing a pair of soft, well-worn, cream-colored jeans and nothing else. His feet and chest were bare.

At the startled look in her eyes, he said quickly, "The security guard rang me to tell me you were on your way up." He took her arm. "Come in."

He led her into the living room, a place done in shades of burgundy and a rich blue with a soft, deep couch and too many throw rugs scattered about on top of white carpeting. There were pillows on the floor with fringed tassels and pillows on the sofa. The place made her think of an apartment a sultan would insist on if he moved into a New York condominium. Luc had obviously been sitting in one corner of the couch. It was cleared of pillows, and a glass filled with some amber liquid sat on a small square table in a direct right angle. Beside the glass lay a yellow legal pad, the first page full of writing, and a ball-point pen. Tools of the trade.

"I tried to call you," Luc said, leading her toward the couch. "I wanted to warn you."

She sat down in the velvety softness, feeling suddenly very warm in the air-conditioned coolness.

He said, "What can I get you to drink?"

"Nothing. Luc, I—"

Arrested, he turned toward her. "What is it, Rana?" He moved a pillow and sat down beside her.

She ran her hand over the velvet arm of the couch, so aware of his hard thigh close to hers that her skin burned. She looked away from him. "I don't want"—the words seemed to be lodged in her throat—"I don't want—" She turned to him, her eyes blazing. "My God, why did you go on that show?"

Her burst of anger threw him off-balance. He leaned back slightly, away from her. "It's in my contract that if my pub-

70

lisher wants me to do publicity for a book, I do it. I had no choice, Rana."

"Stop fighting my battles," she said through clenched teeth.

"You weren't there to fight them. What was I supposed to do? Throw you to the wolves?"

"Yes. Yes!" She shot up off the couch to whirl around and face him. "After what I did to you, how could you possibly sit there and defend me?"

He stared at her in stunned silence. "Oh, God." She whirled away from him. "Don't make me—"

"Don't make you what, Rana?" he probed, his tone deceptively soft.

"Don't make me . . . feel anything for you. I don't want to." Aware that he hadn't moved, she turned back to him. "I can't, don't you see that?"

He leaned back and laid one arm along the couch, tipping his head to look up at her. His bare chest gleamed in the soft light. For a man who was dark, he wasn't overly endowed with body hair. His chest was lightly covered with hair in the center, but the tanned skin along his waistline was bare.

His eyes met hers, read them. "I think it's too late for that. You already feel something for me"—his voice went a shade softer—"or you wouldn't be here right now looking at me that way."

"It's only physical attraction," she murmured, thinking she was denying everything, not really aware of how much she was admitting.

That faint, wonderful, devastating smile appeared at the corner of his lips. "The judges will accept that"—he didn't move—"until the contestant has done more study in the subject area."

He stood up and carefully, as if he were handling glass, put his hands on her shoulders to draw her closer.

"It can't last." She felt as if she were underwater, her muscles gone slack with relaxation, surrounded by a sea of warm liquid. "I'll hurt you. I've already caused you pain. . . ."

71

"If you really feel that sorry for me, come closer . . . and give me something to make all my suffering worthwhile."

"Luc . . ."

He dropped his mouth lightly over her eyelashes, her nose, her cheeks. "Rich man, poor man, beggarman, thief." He bent and ran his lips over the bared hollow of her throat. "Doctor, lawyer, Indian chief. Did you play that jump rope game when you were a little girl to see what kind of man your lover would be? Bet when they said writer, you were very careful not to miss a single step, weren't you, Rana O'Neill?"

"It was never one of the choices." Her voice shook. "It never *has* been one of the choices."

"But life throws us some strange curves. And you're here, in my apartment, in my arms . . . of your own choice, Rana."

"My mother destroyed my father," she said in a blunt, stark tone.

"How old are you?"

The question didn't make any sense. He smiled at her as if he understood her confusion and repeated the question in that gentle tone that cajoled and teased.

"Twenty-nine," she told him, finally.

"Far too old."

"Too old . . . for what?" Her puzzlement amused him even more.

"Too old to be a clone of your mother," he said matter-of-factly. "And I don't think"—a hand came up to trace lightly down her cheek—"I'm very much like your father."

Oh, but you are, she thought desperately. *You are. You are a dangerous, attractive man that half the women in the world would like to wake up beside in the morning, and your charm is only exceeded by your keen brain and your six-figure advances.*

The finger wandered lower and discovered the outline of her jaw. She said, "You know what happened . . . between them. You must see that I can't risk hurting you—"

"There's more risk in my wringing your neck if you don't stop saying those stupid things and let me show you something much more interesting to do with that mouth of yours." He covered her lips with his, offering her no quarter, thrusting his tongue deeply into the softness of her mouth that was half-open to him, lifting her tongue with his. His hands were warm and sure on her back, traveling lightly, one pressing her shoulders against him, the other cupping the warm roundness of her bottom and pressing her hips into his. His chest, warm, hard, a man's chest, nudged her breasts. She smelled cedar and felt silk and burned and ached in ways she had never known possible.

He pressed her downward into the velvet cushions, his mouth still on hers, his arms cradling her against the fall.

He lifted his mouth. "And I thought Kensington was crazy when he bought this huge sofa. Velvet no less. Now I see that he was very farsighted." He moved, catching her legs at the ankles and bringing them up to rest on top of the cushion. "Very farsighted indeed."

"Will you know what to say?" she asked dryly.

He drew back, his brows drawn together. "What?"

"This isn't quite the right setting for a standard seduction scene from a Luc Garrett western. Don't your men usually make love to their women in a covered wagon or beside a forest stream?"

His blue eyes played over her. "This isn't a standard seduction scene from anybody's book."

"What is it then?"

"It's me," he said softly, "me discovering you. And you"—he brought her hands up to his bare chest—"you discovering me."

"You seem like a fairly normal specimen." Her tone was light, flippant, her heart rocketing. She put a palm on his shoulder where tendon ran from arm to chest and tested it lightly with her fingertips. "All of your puzzle parts are assembled in the normal way." His skin felt warm under her hands and vibrantly alive.

"How can you be sure?" he drawled mockingly. "You haven't investigated . . . thoroughly."

He shifted slightly, forcing her to slide her palms higher to keep him from lowering his weight on her, and her hands discovered more curly-crisp hair and the male nipples underneath. The hard buds bloomed under her touch.

She should move her hands away, she knew she should, but . . . he felt so good, so good.

"Yes," he said, and she knew he could see her eyes darkening, changing, feel her fingers curling into him, see the flush rising just under her chin, her own body undergoing the subtle changes that told him she was not indifferent to him.

Hold back, Garrett. For God's sake, be careful. This lady requires very careful handling. If you try to take her head on, you'll lose her.

She was wearing a silk blouse and a linen skirt, and he could feel the silky fabric and the slim buckle of that neat, narrow belt she wore pressing into his bare skin. "I think," he murmured, "I'd be more comfortable if you'd take off your clothes."

She laughed, just as he had hoped she would, and put her hand up to his cheek, as he hadn't dreamed she would dare.

Her smile lingering, she said, "Why is it I'm not afraid of you?"

He went very still, savoring the touch of her fingers on his jaw. "Because you can deck me?" he said helpfully, smiling down at her.

She laughed again, softly, her voice low and husky. "You overplayed that just a little, you know."

He drew back, his eyes widening. "Overplayed it?"

She pushed at him, and to her surprise, he sat up and eased his weight off of her. She was still quite effectively trapped because he sat on the outside of the sofa while she lay on the inside, almost drowning in the velvet cushions.

She said, "It all seemed too easy. You were too . . . off guard. After all, you had initiated the contest. It wasn't as if I had gone after you. I . . . well, Clem had this strange look in his eyes and I . . . I called him the next day. That was when he told me you had taught self-defense when you were in the service."

74

"I'm going to have to speak to Clem about the size of his mouth."

"Why should he lie? Luc, what are you trying to prove?"

He hesitated for a moment and then got to his feet. The warmth on the side of her hip where his body had pressed against hers was gone. He went to a small table that sat against the wall behind the couch that held a crystal decanter and some glasses. "Would you care for something?"

She shook her head, and as if he had expected her refusal, he poured himself a drink. He took a swallow and then looked at her as she sat twisted around on the sofa, watching him.

"It's not very complicated, really. I simply didn't want to embarrass you."

"So you embarrassed yourself instead."

"I'm not easily embarrassed."

"But I've embarrassed you with my columns."

"Going to retract them?" he asked, watching her.

She felt chilled suddenly. "Is that what you want from me?"

"What makes you think I want something from you?"

"Luc, don't pull your punches with me. If you want me to write a retraction, say so."

He held up his glass and looked at her. "Somehow I don't think it's quite that simple."

"What . . . do you mean?"

"The sales of my next book will very probably be down—thanks to you."

Her skin prickled. "You don't really believe that."

"I don't say things I don't believe."

He meant it.

"I can't believe I've done the great Lucas Garrett that much damage. People simply don't buy or not buy a book on the strength of what one person might say—"

"I'm not talking about the people buying my book. I'm talking about my ability to write it." He leaned back against the table. "You've said my women characters aren't right. How the hell do you think I'm going to be able to sit down and create an effective heroine now? You've very subtly, but very effectively, undermined my ability to do that."

"I don't believe you." She felt icy, desolate, suddenly very alone in a room where only moments before she had felt Luc Garrett's body come to life under her hands.

"Don't you? You should. You're a writer. You know that it doesn't take much to set up a nice little block. And that's what you've done, lady."

"If that's true," she murmured, "I should think you wouldn't have let me off so easily the other day at Clem's party. It's a wonder you didn't strangle me."

He looked at her for a moment. In the quiet of the apartment, the air, that cool air pumped out in efficient rhythm by the air conditioner, hummed with an electricity that stretched across the room from Luc's bare-chested body to hers. He said softly, "That wasn't the thought that immediately occurred to me at the time . . . and it's not what I'm thinking about now."

She went icy-hot with anger and another disturbing emotion she didn't want to name. "You defend me in public at the expense of your dignity—but in private, you have no compunction at all about slicing me into ribbons, do you, Mr. Garrett?"

"Cutting you to ribbons? Is that what you call it?" He turned away suddenly for the overt purpose of setting his glass on the table, but she had the feeling that he was far more interested in keeping his face hidden from her.

The velvet couch became confining, and she rose out of the luxurious prison, her one thought to escape while her reeling mind and body were still functioning.

He turned back and eyed her from under heavy lids.

The atmosphere was too electric, too—real. She cried, "You really do want revenge, don't you?"

"Actually, no." He pushed himself away from the table. "Revenge is the last thing on my mind at the moment." He waited, and when she didn't reply, he took a step toward her. "Strange as it may seem, I'm trying to come up with a way to ask you to stay the night with me . . . but . . ." He shrugged, that attractive, self-mocking smile lifting his mouth. "At this—of all times—I don't seem to have the right words."

"A prescribed cure for writer's block?" she asked.

He took another step. "I only know that if you walk out that door, I will be more lonely than I have ever been in my life."

She stood frozen, unable to move.

He moved toward her again. He still wasn't very close and the couch was between them and she told herself it wasn't dangerous to stand there, eating him with her eyes, but she knew it was. Her mind urged her to move, but her body was wiser; she burned to feel the touch of his hands. And so she did nothing. She felt as if he were a million miles away . . . yet every cell in her body was aware of him, the gleam of light off his dark hair, the bronzed glow of his chest, the glitter in his eyes, eyes that never left her face.

From across the two feet of room that separated them, his desire, his need, reached out to her. "Stay, Rana."

The silence stretched.

"No," she whispered at last. "I can't."

He stood very still for a second, and then he came around the couch with a swift lunge that caught her off guard.

She moved, but not quickly enough. He clasped her upper arms with his hard hands and stopped her headlong flight as easily as if she were a child, bringing her around to face him.

"I swore I wasn't going to do this," he said in a hoarse voice. "I swore I wasn't going to use force to make you listen to reason—"

"Reason." She lifted her head and met his eyes, her own tear-brilliant. "This isn't reason. It's insanity."

"You've got to let go of the past. You've got to forget—"

"Forget that my mother killed my father?"

Her blunt words stopped him for a moment, threw him off-balance. He stared at her, then collected himself and shook his head. He said, "That's not true. He'd had too much to drink. He went off the road in a place where there had been several accidents before. . . ."

77

She put her hands on his waist, bracing herself against him. "You weren't there. You didn't hear them arguing before he went out. . . ." She stopped, her words caught in her throat. Then, as if she couldn't stop herself, the words began to spill out again. "It was a game they played, a stupid, cruel game. They didn't even realize they were hurting each other—or me—until it was too late."

He'd read the details in the paper, of course, along with the rest of the world. John O'Neill, famous playwright and author, dead at the age of fifty-two. His wife, a witty and articulate critic whose column was syndicated in over a hundred papers around the country, had taken an overdose of sleeping pills soon after the accident. Years before, they were the golden couple. Their marriage had been glamorized and written up in several of the tabloids until recently, when they started battling, in public and in private. The press cataloged each step of the breakdown of their marriage, until their life together was likened by one of the bright young reporters of the theater crowd as a long-playing scene from *Who's Afraid of Virginia Woolf?*

Filled with pity and desire and a deep frustration, he said, "Is this your mother's body I'm holding?"

"No," she said softly, very softly, "but there's a part of her mind in my head that I live with every day of my life." Her fingers tightened around his waist, as if every word caused her pain. "That's why I took up karate. I thought it would teach me control, control of my mind, control of my body."

"And has it?"

"Only partially. Sometimes I forget that I can't ever really care about anyone—"

"Don't think about caring," he said in a strange tone. "Don't think about love. Think about touching me, holding me. Think about having someone around to share your thoughts and your kisses and your bed. . . ."

He stood so close, a banquet of forbidden fruit, and in her agony and loneliness she leaned forward to take a small taste. He stood quiescent under her kiss, awarding her the initiative, letting her mouth explore his, the only sign of his heightened tension the tightening of his hands on her arms.

His control was an elemental challenge she couldn't resist. She nibbled and teased and stroked him with her tongue, discovering the taste of the brandy he had just drunk, taking the scent of him from his mouth to hers, forgetting everything in her need to experience the deep, primitive comfort of kissing a man she adored. She melted against him.

He moved away from her slightly, wincing a little. "That belt buckle. Rana, let me . . ."

His hands brushed over her breast, their ultimate goal the buttons on her blouse. Those warm fingers began to undress her, and the touch of those slightly calloused tips against her soft flesh brought her to the stinging realization that Luc wasn't playing. He wanted to make love to her, and she had done nothing to stop him. Quite the opposite. She had kissed him, stroked him with her tongue, and now her silence and stillness were giving him tacit permission to do just what he was doing. . . .

She pulled away, out of his reach.

She saw the effort it took for him to stay where he was and not come after her. She saw the clench of his jaw, his hands. He leashed his body, his control an almost visible thing. But there were things he couldn't hide. He couldn't hide the glitter in his eyes—or the arousal of his body. For a long silent moment she heard nothing but his breathing—and hers. Then he said, "Are you deliberately trying to drive me up the wall?"

"I shouldn't have come."

"There's an understatement of magnificent proportion. Now the real question is"—those blue eyes fastened on hers—"do I keep you with me . . . or let you go?"

"You're going to let me go, Luc. Because you understand. Because you know it's best . . . for both of us."

He was still, more still than she had ever seen him. His vibrant, restless energy was frozen behind an unsmiling countenance. He said, "I'm supposed to let the one woman who has ever bothered to look beyond the facade of my life walk out on me?"

"I can't—don't do this to me." A hard, unrelenting pain twisted inside of her. "Don't make me feel responsible."

"You are responsible. You—"

She shook her head. "I—"

The sharp buzz of the doorbell jangled through her nervous system wildly.

Luc stared at her. She said, "You have company. I'd better go—"

"No, you wait." The buzzer went again, more impatiently this time. Luc made a sound of displeasure. "It had better not be anyone I know." His face dark, he walked around her toward the door.

A petite redhead stood outside, her hair tousled, her eyes wide and dark with fatigue and some other emotion Rana couldn't name. The newcomer didn't see Rana. Those dark, young-old eyes saw only Luc. After a brief hesitation, the young woman stepped into Luc's arms. "I'm sorry," she said in a muffled voice. "I had to come."

"Karin. What—"

She shook her head. "Don't ask. Just . . . hold me for a minute, will you? I've missed you."

His hands, the hands that only a moment ago had dealt so competently with the buttons of her blouse, came up to hold the girl, his arms offering her a shelter from the storm she carried inside her.

Luc turned, still holding the girl, for she was a girl, really, perhaps nineteen or twenty, as she cried softly into his chest. "This is an old friend from home, Karin Hughes. Her father owns a neighboring ranch in Wyoming."

"Yes, I see." She dropped her eyes, willing herself to look away from that bright flame of hair pressed to the bare skin of Luc's chest. "I really must go."

At the sound of her voice, the girl in Luc's arms lifted her head. She looked from Rana to Luc, saw the expression on his face, and pulled away from him. "I'm intruding. I should have known you'd have someone with you. I'll find a motel—"

Luc had no compunction about using force on this girl. He caught her arm in a grip that made the girl wince. "You're not going anywhere. Not until I find out why you're in New York."

Rana stiffened slightly at the girl's easy acceptance of her presence. Evidently the girl knew Luc very well, well enough not to expect him to go without female attention for any extended period of time.

Over the top of the girl's head Rana's eyes met Luc's. At first, all she saw was anger. Then suddenly, those blue eyes took on a curious gleam, a strangely disturbing glow. Perhaps Luc loved this girl.

Rana forced the sick feeling back at the pit of her throat and moved toward the door. "Excuse me—"

"There's no reason for you to leave," he rapped out.

She shook her head. "I think there is. You . . . look as if you have your hands full."

She brushed past him, and as she reached the door, she heard the girl protesting once again, telling Luc that she would go to a motel, and Luc's sharp command to forget it.

When the door closed, Karin Hughes pushed herself out of Luc's arms, lifted her head, sniffed once, and ran a hand through the long mane of her hair. "Swell. Now I've ruined your love life, too."

He remembered the look on Rana's face when he'd taken Karin into his arms. Was that jealousy he saw in her eyes? If it was, Karin's interruption was well worth any price. "Maybe not. What are you doing here, squirrel?"

Karin lifted an elegant shoulder. "Can't you guess? Me and my mouth. I got so sick of it, trying to get Con to look at me as a woman, trying to convince him that this crush I'm supposed to have on you is a figment of his imagination."

"Where's your bag?"

"I don't have one," she said defiantly. "Con made me so

angry that I told him I didn't need to go home and pack, that you'd buy me what I need."

"Living very dangerously these days aren't you, my pretty red squirrel?"

She stopped pacing the floor and looked at him. "It's not living," she said in a very adult tone.

"Did anyone ever tell you you're one spoiled brat?"

"Only you and Con, a dozen times a day since the day I was old enough to stand up."

"What makes you think you should get what you want when you want it?"

"The one thing I've always wanted I've never had." She gazed at him out of brown eyes that held so much pain he almost thought for a moment that a stranger was standing there. Disturbed, he fell back on the old lines, the familiar lines.

"You're too young to marry Con. You've got to finish college, see something of the world." Luc paused. "Grow up."

"I'm 'up,' " she said through gritted teeth.

"Not to Con you're not."

"I never will be to him. I'll always be the little kid in pigtails who tagged after him while he fixed fence." She sighed.

"I wonder why," he murmured. "How did you pay for your airline ticket?"

She looked up at him with guileless brown eyes. "With Dad's credit card."

"So in other words, some other person—a responsible, working adult—financed your little temper tantrum."

"If you're going to start preaching to me—"

"I think it's about time somebody did. You think about that while I see if I can find a place for you to stay the night."

"You mean I'm not staying here?"

"No," said Luc firmly, "you're not staying here."

"You're not going to put me out on the street, are you?"

"Don't tempt me," Luc warned, going to the rotary file he kept by the telephone and wondering if he would be rousing Helen and Clem out of bed.

He turned back to Karin. "And as soon as I've made my call, I want you to call your father and tell him you arrived safely."

Chastised, she said, "I did that at the airport."

Luc gazed at her. "Well, maybe there is hope for you after all."

CHAPTER FIVE

The next morning Rana told her computer the fact that a beautiful young girl had landed on Luc's doorstep last night didn't mean anything to her. She wasn't interested. She couldn't be interested. Luc Garrett was the last person in the world she would ever be interested in. And just when she had almost convinced herself of that fact, and had settled down to write, the phone rang—and the breathless voice on the other end of the line identified herself as Karin Hughes.

"Ms. O'Neill? I wanted to call and apologize for breaking in on you last night."

"You don't have to apologize."

"Well, maybe not, but . . . I wanted to anyway. I'm trying to"—Rana heard the girl breathe inward deeply—"I'm trying to act like a responsible adult. Clem and Helen gave me your number. They said it would be all right if I called you. They said you wouldn't mind. I . . . hope you don't. Are you busy writing?"

"Not right at the moment," she said, unable to keep the dryness out of her tone.

"I stayed with Clem and Helen last night. I . . . wanted you to know that."

She didn't know what to say to that. She heard the girl take a breath. "Luc is my friend. Nothing more."

"You don't have to explain yourself to me, Miss Hughes."

"Please, I'd . . . I'd like you to call me Karin. Well, I . . . I hope I see you again before I leave New York."

"Thank you." She was stricken with guilt. If she had known,

85

she could have told Luc to let the girl stay with her. But she hadn't known. She had thought—no, she hadn't been thinking at all. She had been feeling raw, painful feelings. She hadn't been thinking. If she had, she would have wondered what brought this girl running to Luc with pain in her eyes. "Would you care to have lunch with me one day this week?"

Karin's voice warmed instantly. "I'd love to."

"How about tomorrow?"

"Tomorrow will be great—if Luc doesn't throw me back on a plane today."

"We'll have to see to it that he doesn't do that."

"He thinks he's more liberal-minded than his brother about women, but he's just as bad." Without taking a breath, she said, "I've been reading your columns. They're very good." There was a pause. "For the first time in my life, you made me think about Luc from the inside out, do you know what I mean?"

"Yes, I think I know what you mean."

"Well, I'd better let you go. I'll see you tomorrow then. Where will I meet you?"

"Why don't you get in a taxi and come here and we'll decide where we want to go when you arrive?"

"Sounds super."

They said other things, the polite things that people say when they are ringing off a conversation. Rana replaced the phone and had just gone back to her computer to stare in frustration at the screen and try to get her thoughts coordinated when, a few minutes later, the phone rang again.

"Rana? You see Luc Garrett on the Dave Hartley show last night?"

Rana twisted the phone cord in her hand, bracing herself for whatever might come. It was Sam Martin, the head of the syndicate, the man she alternately loved and hated, a man she didn't take orders from but rather listened to. "Yes. What about it?"

"He stirred up speculation about the two of you all over

again. Give us another column about him, will you, Rana? Right now the two of you are hot copy."

She tortured the phone cord, wishing it were Sam's neck she was twisting. "No, Sam."

Gruffly, Sam came back, "What do you mean, 'No, Sam'?"

"I mean no, I'm not going to do another column about him."

Shrewdly, Sam countered, "Why not?"

"I've said all I have to say on the subject of Luc Garrett." Her voice took on a darker color when she said Luc's name. She could only pray Sam hadn't heard it, too.

Sam drawled, "Have you now?" She could almost see him, leaning back in his chair, closing his eyes, thinking. Why was the newspaper business filled with men as sharp and shrewd as old sea lions?

"Yes, I have. The subject is closed."

There was a silence. "All right, Rana. I'll let you go on this one."

Canny Sam. He had no other choice. Her contract gave her complete control over the content of her column. It was up to each individual paper whether they used her stuff or not. She hung up the phone, thinking it was nice of Sam to magnanimously grant her what she already had—and wondered what in the devil she would have done if he had decided to apply more pressure.

After that, the day disintegrated. She got another call from a girl she had gone to Smith with and five minutes later a wrong number. In desperation she hooked her recording machine onto the line. After that she managed to get some work done.

She finished the column that afternoon. She had the feeling it wasn't one of her better efforts, but it was done.

That evening when she went to take a bath, the recording machine was still on. She had left it on, thinking it would be good just to relax in the tub and not have to worry about answering the phone. Just as she had stripped and was ready to step into the froth of bubbles, she heard the phone ring, heard her own recorded message, heard Luc's terse voice saying, "If there's anything I hate, it's talking to a damn machine," and the sharp click of the receiver.

Naked at the edge of the tub, she wavered indecisively. She could either go out and return Luc's call now while her nerves were still singing in reaction to hearing his voice, or she could take a bath and try to relax and restore her nerves and then return his call. But how could she relax when she would be wondering why he had called?

She reached for her robe.

She punched out Luc's number and let the phone ring repeatedly. No answer. Maybe he'd been out when he called.

She went back to her cooling bathwater feeling faintly anxious, knowing she had no right to be. Luc had probably agreed to take Karin out for the evening and had tried to reach her before he left.

She got out of the tub, donned her terry robe, and ran a hand through the loose fall of her brown hair. She was thinking she should get into her leotard and do her exercises when the doorbell rang.

She hesitated and then went to answer it with the chain lock on. When she saw one half of Luc's face, she slipped the chain.

He came into the room angrily, bringing a blast of warm air with him from the hallway. She closed the door to keep the air conditioner from kicking in and said, "Hello, Luc."

She felt very warm suddenly, dressed in that terry robe. She leaned back against the door, her hands finding the ridge of wood in the middle. She couldn't think why he was here. Actually, she was having trouble thinking at all. The sight of Luc, cool and compact in a white linen shirt with the sleeves rolled up and black denim pants that were body-molded to his thighs was enough to destroy any woman's concentration.

He stood inches away from her, his brows furrowed in anger, his tension reaching out to her and raising the fine hairs on her arms. Why had she ever had the nerve to think she could challenge him, either physically or mentally?

"You're a difficult woman to get hold of."

Defiant, somehow wanting to deny the effect he had on her just by coming into a room, she headed straight into the fire. "How much of a hold do you want on me, Mr. Garrett?"

She already had her back to the door, and when he stepped closer, she had nowhere to go. He stared at her for a moment and then said coolly, watching her, "I think you know the answer to that question."

"Do I?" Her blood churned through her veins. Like a trapped animal, she watched his every move, knowing she was flying high on the voltage his presence in the apartment generated.

He said, "You do it on purpose, don't you?"

"Do what on purpose?" She lifted her chin and faced him, her eyes sparkling with the excitement of meeting him head on.

"Antagonize me." His blue eyes fastened on hers with pinpoint precision.

"Not on purpose."

"That's what you'd like to believe, isn't it?" In a softer tone, "That's what you'd like to believe yourself. But when I touch you"—he reached out and with a fingertip, found the hollow of her throat, and then traced slowly down the collar of her robe along her warm, scented skin—"we both know it's exactly what you want."

She wanted desperately to deny his words, to move away, to repudiate his claim of ownership. But he was watching her too closely. She could only stand and let the shivery excitement course through her veins, her own fingers aching to reach out, catch those well-shaped wrists, turn his hand over and run her tongue over his palm.

Luc saw every one of the response signals of her body. The way her breathing altered as his finger went lower, the flush deepening at the base of her throat; the dark expansion of her eyes brought a deep, elemental satisfaction—and responses of his own.

"You think you're outside of my world, safe. But you're not," he said, his other hand taking both ends of the belt of her robe and using it to pull her toward him. "You're not safe, Rana. Not anymore."

His kiss was light, a mere brush of his lips on hers. He had to be careful yet, so careful. He had to take the risk, venture into foreign territory, try for the golden prize of intimacy before he took the sweet, silver promise of her body. They were halfway there already. She'd talked to him about her parents, and Clem had told him she'd never done that with anyone before. But he wanted more, had to have more, and so he was going to give more—of himself. If she didn't accept his gift, he would be left with a residue of pain too powerful to think about. "Go get dressed. You're going out with me."

Going out? She hadn't expected that. "No, Luc—"

He looped the terry belt over his hand and held her as he might have a tethered calf. His mouth just over hers, he said softly, "You'd rather stay here?"

"You know that's not what I meant."

"You started this whole thing by telling me exactly what you meant, word by incisive word. Don't stop now."

"I want you to leave—"

"I intend to," he said smoothly, "with you. Just as soon as you are suitably dressed to go out. Of course"—he paused, and that wonderful, damnable smile lifted his lips—"we do have the alternative of staying in and doing something suited to the way you're dressed."

"You're making me wish I really could throw you two falls out of three."

"That's exactly what I had in mind," he said silkily.

Pulses pounding, she pulled her belt free of his grip. He let it go. She pivoted and escaped to the bedroom, closing the door firmly behind her. The safest thing to do was to leave the apartment as soon as possible. Whatever he had in mind couldn't be as dangerous as standing so close to him that she could feel the subtle press of bone and muscle through terry cloth, and, worse, the leap of her own body in response.

She emerged minutes later, her hair tied back demurely in a

leather clasp, her body still heated under a soft peasant blouse and a full, crinkly cotton skirt in a color of brown that matched her hair and floated to a point below her knees, almost touching the thongs of her Roman sandals that wound around her legs.

He rose from the carpet block he'd been sitting on with that easy grace he had and moved forward, taking her arm as if he had a perfect right to do so.

"You didn't say where we were going, so I wasn't exactly sure how to dress."

He smiled at her, making her feel prim and just a little foolish. "You're very appropriate—for any occasion."

"You make me feel like a greeting card," she shot back, knowing her cheeks were coloring again.

"Is that what I make you feel like?"

She shook her head. He followed her out and leaned against the wall while she locked the door.

Outside the building she stepped into the night that was still sticky with heat and slid across the seat of the taxi, leaving half her skirt behind her. Luc brushed it aside and followed her in to settle himself beside her.

"Is it against the rules to tell me where you're taking me?"

"Where would anyone take a greeting card?" he mocked her softly. "To the post office, of course, after the envelope is sealed. . . ." He picked up her hand and brought it to his mouth, touching her palm lightly with the tip of his tongue.

A sensual shiver glided over her skin, cool against the heat. She tugged at her hand. Luc chuckled softly and cradled her fingers against his thigh, his hand hard and warm on top of hers.

Manhattan slid by on a dark, warm blanket of dreams and blinking lights and the ever-present sound of car horns. The cabbie, as taciturn as any, threaded his way through the traffic to a part of the city she knew to be the home of Off Broadway, the recently renovated section known as the Forty-second Street Theater Row. The car stopped, Luc paid the driver, opened the door, and helped her out.

91

There were no lights on the front of the small theater that Luc guided her toward.

"I don't think—"

"Relax. Trust me."

You don't know what you're asking, she thought. Yet perhaps he did. His hand on her elbow was gentle.

He plucked a set of keys out of his pocket and unlocked the door.

"We're going into an empty theater?"

"It won't be empty when we're in it."

That was the kind of Lucian logic she was beginning to know well—and worse, understand.

Luc knew exactly where all the light switches were. He flipped them on one by one, illuminating a small lobby where the walls were covered with pictures of the great actresses and actors of the last fifty years, the sultry Bette Davis, Alfred Lunt, Richard Burton, Laurence Olivier costumed as Hamlet, holding up a cross with the look of fanatic dedication to the tortured vision in his mind.

"Come inside," Luc said.

She followed him into a darkened theater, the finger of light from the lobby gleaming on the sculptured thickness of his brown hair. In the dim light, she saw that there weren't many seats, at the most, she guessed, one hundred. The house was something like the old, intimate Princess Theatre, in which Jerome Kern produced his first fledgling musicals.

From the papers lying in a haphazard pile on a back seat, Luc picked up a sheet and handed it to her. In the light from the lobby door she saw it was a rehearsal schedule. Names, dates, times, and a final production date of October 22. At the top, the name of the play was *A Time of Ungreatness*. The playwright's name was Lucas Garrett.

"This is actually the reason I came to Manhattan."

He left her standing there with the rehearsal schedule in her hand and walked away from her down the aisle. In the semi-darkness he climbed the steps easily and disappeared behind the soft cheesecloth curtain. She heard a heavy, hard click, and in the next instant the stage was bathed in light. And so was Luc.

The set was bare of furniture. None was needed. Luc, walking to the center, commanded her attention with a vividness that swept everything else away. Slowly, he turned to face her, his hands thrust in the pockets of his pants. "The ultimate ego trip. Writing words for other people to say. I lie awake at night and wonder if I'm crazy, trying this after so many years of working in another field."

He looked over the empty seats at her. "I would have introduced you to the cast," he said, that faint, soul-destroying smile lifting his lips, "but one of the principal actresses became ill and they finished early tonight."

Under the conventional words, electricity pulsed. A silence permeated the theater, a silence that held whispers of dreams. Luc's dreams. "Do you think I'm crazy, Rana?"

She felt as if she couldn't breathe, couldn't move.

He turned toward her slightly, letting the light play over his face. Even spotlighted as he was, his body moved with the easy sureness of a man who'd lived and worked out of doors. She could see him completely. And yet she was hidden in the shadowy outer darkness.

This wasn't fair, she thought, agonized. This just wasn't fair. She didn't want to know his secrets. She didn't want to know him.

He waited in that aching silence, waited for her words.

Out of a tight throat in the lightest tone she could manage, she said, "I won't know until I see the play, will I?"

He didn't move a muscle. "No advance prejudices about a western hack writer trying to write a serious play?"

"I try not to have advance prejudices," she said, still striving for lightness, "and you are not a hack writer."

"There are those who think I am. They'll be waiting for me to fall on my face. Will you come with me on opening night and hold my hand?"

She looked down at the schedule. October 22. "Yes," she said softly. "I'll hold your hand."

He didn't move from the stage. "And what about the time in between, Rana?" He stood still, so very still. "Will you hold my hand during the time in between?"

Her chest felt heavy. Her heart pounded against her breastbone at twice the normal rate. The silence stretched, expanded, took on life of its own. And in that silence that curled around and between them like fog, she said the one thing that had eaten at the back of her mind since she walked into the theater. "My father . . . my father must have started out in a theater just like this. He must have had such high hopes . . . just like you. . . ."

To her own ears her voice sounded cool and detached. But Luc heard the pain.

He cursed himself for a fool. It hadn't even occurred to him that bringing her here would only compound the coincidental parallel of his career with her father's. He'd thought only of sharing the dream of his life with her. Instead, he had brought about his own destruction.

He'd gambled . . . and he'd lost.

He stood on that stage with the lights blazing down on him and felt raw and exposed. He steeled himself against the pain and turned and walked across the stage, his face and arms burning from the heat of the stage lights, heat that he hadn't felt during that time when his whole concentration was on Rana. He reached for the breaker switch and threw it to the off position, feeling as if he'd done the same thing to his life.

She waited for him out in the lobby, next to the picture of Bette Davis, her teeth clenched, her body shivering in the heavy heat.

It has to be this way. It must be this way. There is no future for us. He's safer away from me. He'll write, he'll work . . . and he'll stay alive. I won't destroy him.

Twenty minutes later the taxi pulled over to the curb in front of Rana's apartment house.

"Wait for me," Luc told the driver.

"You don't have to walk me to the door, Luc."

"I want to," he said in a cold, desolate voice that made her think he was anxious to get rid of her, anxious to close this chapter of his life.

The temperature hadn't dropped. The night was still sultry. Heat radiated up from the sidewalk at her as she stepped out of the car.

In the shelter of the entryway, he pulled her into his arms. "Luc—"

"What makes you think you can have everything your own way?" he said roughly. "The balance of power has shifted. It's all on your side. I want something back, Rana, something to take with me." He brought his mouth down on hers, and for the first time, she felt his desperate need for a response from her. His mouth demanded and his tongue probed relentlessly.

In the next instant she was free. He twisted on his heel and went, leaving her standing there to watch him slide lithely into the cab and disappear into the night.

Inside her apartment a few minutes later, she undressed for bed, words circling like restless gulls in her brain.

I lie awake at night and wonder if I'm crazy . . . do you think I'm crazy, Rana? The balance of power has shifted. It's all on your side.

Luc's words echoed in her head, his kiss lingered with silky sweetness on her mouth. *Oh, Luc. Please get out of my life!*

He sprawled on the velvet couch, a glass of alcoholic antidote in his hand, the bottle of scotch within easy reach on the table beside him. He tossed back a long, deep swallow and felt the liquor burn a bitter trail over his tongue.

He set the glass on the table very carefully. *Have to be careful with glasses. They break. Have to be careful with people. They*

95

break, too. Have to be careful with Rana O'Neill. Can't push her around like you do the people in your head.

His stomach twisted.

Just tell her what's important to you, you told yourself. Just open up your life and let her in. And she'll let you into hers.

Biggest piece of fiction you've ever hatched up.

He picked up the glass, drank again, balanced the glass on his knee, and laid his head awkwardly back on the low, supporting cushion behind him.

A bargain. I give this much of myself to you, Rana O'Neill, and you give this much of yourself back. . . .

A poor bargain, Garrett. A damn poor bargain.

He lifted the glass again. She didn't buy it, Garrett. Not any of it. She tossed your little revelation neatly back in your face and said no thank-you very much.

Now what are you going to do?

First order of business: stop thinking. No more thinking. Thinking is bad for the brain . . . and the soul . . . and the heart.

At the Grand Hyatt Hotel the next day, Karin sat across from Rana in the Sungarden Lounge and enthused about everything. Her face aglow with pleasure, she enjoyed the food, the atmosphere, and watching the people bustling along on the sidewalk below them. Her bubbling voice and animated face made Rana feel old. Maybe she'd been in New York too long. Maybe she needed to get away. Maybe she needed a sanctuary—

"—and so I tried to call Luc, but he didn't answer."

All Rana's nerves came to life. Striving for a casual tone, she said, "When was that?"

"This morning." Karin plucked a grape from the fruit on her plate and popped it in her mouth. "I thought maybe you might know where he is."

"No. No, I don't."

"He must have been dreaming up some far-out plot and

didn't want to answer the phone. He doesn't usually do that, though."

"Doesn't he?" Rana murmured.

"Not answer the phone, I mean." She chewed, her green eyes moving over Rana in a thoughtful perusal. "Has he told you anything about his first wife?"

Rana's appetite fled. "Karin, Luc and I really don't have that kind of relationship."

"She was unreal." Karin looked past her to gaze down into the street below. Whatever she was watching had arrested her attention thoroughly. Rana turned slightly and saw that Karin was gazing at the lean figure of a towering male moving up the street. His body had the smooth coordination and the sensual attraction that was eye-catching, but . . . She turned back to her plate, wondering if it was safe to let this child out alone.

"He isn't as good-looking as Conrad."

Startled, Rana stared at her.

"Conrad Garrett. Luc's brother. The man who's driving me crazy. Tina liked him, too."

At Rana's puzzled look, she went on cheerfully, "Luc's wife, Tina. She liked Conrad—but he wasn't the only one. She liked a lot of other men, too. And when she had Luc at home . . ." Karin's voice trailed away momentarily. Then she took a breath and launched into the next phase of her story. "She just couldn't adjust to marriage. There are women, you know, who need more than one man. Tina was one of them."

Inwardly, Rana groaned. Where did this well-read young lady get all her information? From the latest issue of *Playgirl?*

"Tina used a million excuses for going out with other men. She said she had to see other people once in a while. She said it drove her crazy being locked in a house with Luc when all he did was pound the typewriter and mope and read and swear and talk to himself while he thought up stories. She said she married him thinking they'd have a wonderful life together, making the round of the talk shows and going to cocktail parties where people all stood around and admired Luc. But Luc was just starting then; it took him almost ten years to become a best-selling author, and by the time he was, Tina was long gone." The recital stopped, and Karin gazed at her. "What's the matter? Why aren't you eating? Is there something wrong with your food?" The green eyes were wide.

"No. Karin, please, I'd rather you didn't . . . didn't tell me about Luc. I . . . we . . . there's nothing between us."

Karin sat back in the chair and sighed. "Isn't there? I wish there was."

Though she should have known better, she asked, "Why?"

Karin brought her napkin up to blot lips that were young and firm and by now bare of lipstick. Rana wasn't sure whether Karin had eaten her makeup off or talked it off. The young woman moved in her chair and pushed her flame-colored hair back in an unconsciously graceful gesture. "Because a couple of years ago, when Con thought I had a crush on him, I told him I really liked Luc." She rolled her eyes heavenward. "I know, don't tell me. It was a class A stupid thing to do. I didn't realize it at the time, but I do now. Now that I'm old enough for Con to look at, he still believes I have this hang-up about Luc, and he won't touch me. Two days ago we had The Fight Royale, and I told him I was coming out here to see Luc. Once I said that, I couldn't back down, could I?" Heavy lashes came down over expressive eyes. "And that's why I'm here. At least—I think that's why I'm here." A bare shoulder under a narrow spaghetti strap lifted. "Maybe I thought Con would do something to prove that he cared for me. Like stop me from coming." She shook her head and looked away. "He didn't. As far as I'm concerned, the wonderful, wild West cowboy is a big myth." Her full lips twisted. "A myth perpetuated by Luc."

She toyed with her fork. "I liked what you said about him in your columns, did I tell you that? And so did Luc, I think."

"I'm quite sure you're wrong."

"I don't think so. Those articles were really"—she closed her eyes—"right. You know what I mean? They made me think about Luc as a person. Nobody's thought of him as anything but a hunk or a credit card for so long that he probably didn't believe anyone could ever figure him out like that. He's probably fallen in love with you."

"I doubt that—"

"Wouldn't you fall in love with a man that wrote about your life with such clarity?"

"No, and I don't think Luc—"

"—is in love with you? Oh, I think he is. I can't remember when I've ever seen him with a woman and been so sure of anything. The way he looks at you—" She shook her fingers as if she had just touched something too hot to handle.

Rana looked away. How did one deal with such ingenuousness? "Do you like New York City?"

The green eyes examined her. "Are you changing the subject?"

Rana met her scrutiny calmly. "I certainly hope so."

"Luc is a very foxy man. Aren't you interested in him?"

"Karin, please. There are things you don't understand, things . . . I can't explain."

Karin shook her head. "I guess so. I sure don't understand you not wanting Luc."

"It isn't that I don't want him—"

Karin lifted her head, her eyes glowing. "I thought so—"

Appalled at what she had revealed, Rana said hastily, "There's nothing between us. There can't be. Our worlds are miles apart."

Karin murmured something to that; Rana wasn't sure whether it was agreement or disapproval. She finally did manage to guide Karin away from her favorite topic, and the rest of the lunch hour passed peacefully enough, but when they had finished and Rana paid the bill, Karin walked ahead of her down the steps and at the bottom turned around. "I'm going with Luc tonight to watch the rehearsal of his play. Would you like to come along?"

Rana shook her head. "No, thanks. I . . . don't think it would be a good idea."

"Why not?"

"I just don't think it would be." The strain of talking about Luc and of remembering that it was here she had fallen into his arms made her say dryly, "Don't try to matchmake, Karin."

"Somebody needs to do something."

"There's nothing that can be done."

"Are you breaking it off?"

"We never really started—" she stopped. "Yes, I guess I am."

With that familiar impulsiveness, Karin reached out for her hand. "I'm sorry. I think you'd be good for Luc, really I do. He needs someone like you."

Rana shook her head. "No, he doesn't." Her lips lifted. "But thank you for the compliment."

A few minutes later she put Karin in a taxi to take the ride back to Clem's. The girl turned around and waved through the back window as the car pulled away, leaving Rana with a peculiar mixture of relief—and regret.

After she left Karin, Rana went shopping and bought a chair. One chair. It was a huge chair, a big roomy recliner covered in brown leather. The salesman made the arrangements for delivery and told her that because the chair was so big it would take two men for the job, and he made it clear that if she wasn't home when she said she was going to be, she'd have to pay extra to have it delivered twice. She assured him she'd be home when the men came.

She went back to her apartment and stood in the middle of the room and tried to decide where her chair should go. Should she place it by the window so that when the drapes were pulled back she could enjoy a spectacular view of the skyline? Or should it go next to the stereo?

Terry wandered in. He had a key to Rana's apartment, one she had given him long ago so that he could come in and use her computer to play games when she was out during the evening. He had knocked first, and when she called out permission to enter, he came in.

Terry sprawled on a cube. "You bought a chair? What for?"

100

"To sit in, smart guy."

"I thought you didn't like chairs."

"I changed my mind."

"Does this mean you're going to stick around for a while?"

She glanced at him, surprised at the wariness in his tone. Had he been afraid she would walk out of his life—just as his father had?

She strove to be casual. "I suppose it does."

With an elaborate show of boredom, Terry stretched his arms over his head and got to his feet. "Boy, women are sure screwy."

He was needling her on purpose to cover up his own emotions, she knew that. He knew it was like waving a red flag at a bull, and he'd done it on purpose to get a rise out of her—and keep his own feelings from showing. He reminded her a great deal of another sensitive male who tried to hide his vulnerability. . . . "Next time I bake cookies, Clark, yours gets a ration of a toxic substance which may be lethal in nature."

Terry shrugged. "You don't scare me. You're nothing but empty talk, O'Neill."

Am I? Am I really? "I suppose you're right."

Quick as lightning, he caught the half-serious, half-bleak tone in her voice. "Hey. I didn't mean that, you know."

She steeled herself, knowing she had no right to infect Terry with her dull mood. "Get off that cube and move it over two feet, will you? I want to see if I can find a better arrangement."

Terry made a quick recovery from his momentary contriteness. "Nothing doing. If you're going to start moving furniture around, I'm leaving."

"Oh, how fickle is the fair male," she said to his back.

At the door he turned. "Is that a quote?"

"Yes. I just said it, didn't I?"

"I mean, isn't it by anybody famous?"

She clapped a hand over her heart. "You wound me, Clark."

"I think infamous describes you better—"

"And I thought your vocabulary needed expanding." She

picked up a pillow and threw it at him, watching with satisfaction as he yelped and dodged the flying missile. "Get out of here, you smartmouth kid."

Terry let himself out the door.

That evening she locked out thoughts of a darkened theater and a spotlit stage, thoughts of a flame-haired girl who would sit next to Luc's lean, wonderful body and talk to him animatedly, probably all during a scene that Luc wanted to watch, if she knew Karin. And she was beginning to.

In desperation she called on all her powers of concentration and went to sit in front of her computer and tried to put together a column that made sense and that had emotional impact, a column about the chair.

The chair symbolized her capitulation to a need for permanence in her life. She needed something to hang on to. Desperately. Because her world—the world she had constructed so carefully to her own specification—was falling apart. The balance of power had shifted.

"In acting," she wrote, "the actor, when creating a character, tries to touch the things a character would touch, a rose, a book, a knife. He tries to find the house that the character would live in, the furniture that the character would sit on. Because the things that surround us shape our minds—and our lives."

The phone rang. She muttered under her breath that that phone was shaping her life to insanity.

Karin's voice came over the line, breathless, the slow drawl almost gone. "Rana? Have you seen Luc?"

A sudden little flare of alarm leaped along her veins. "No. I thought you were with him."

"I was supposed to be," Karin almost wailed. "I've been waiting and waiting for him to come and pick me up. He's an hour late and he told me what time rehearsal started and it was ages ago. Something's wrong, I know it is."

"Have you tried—"

"—calling his apartment? Yes, of course. I've been ringing

the phone off the wall for the last half hour. I didn't know what to do, and Clem said I should call you."

"I'll . . . see what I can do and get back to you."

She replaced the receiver and went looking for the phone book, her heart beating against her throat. She found the number listed for the security guard at the apartment house where Luc was staying and forced her shaking fingers to punch out the number.

It was the same man who had been there the night she was there, and thank God, he remembered her. No, he hadn't seen Mr. Garrett go out, but he didn't start work until 5:00 that afternoon. Mr. Garrett could have gone out during the day, and he would have no way of knowing it.

"Is there any way to check? Do you know the man who works days? Could you call him?"

The man hesitated. "If it's an emergency, I suppose I could."

"It is," Rana said without hesitation, knowing that Luc would never, under normal circumstances, make a date with Karin and then not let her know that he was unable to keep it.

"I'll see what I can do."

"You'll get back to me right away, one way or another, won't you?"

"You can depend on it, Ms. O'Neill."

In the cool air of her apartment her skin was damp with perspiration. She paced restlessly up and down the carpet in her bare feet. Where was he? What had happened? He was a stranger in the city. For all his expertise, he might have been taken off guard and mugged—or killed. She clasped her arms around herself and shivered. She thought about making herself some coffee, but her stomach rebelled.

The phone rang again, and she ran to answer it.

"I talked to the other man. He says he doesn't remember Mr. Garrett going out, either. I've tried to buzz him, but I can't raise him.

"Couldn't you go to the door and—"

"I wish I could, Miss O'Neill, but I can't leave my post to go up there."

"Yes, of course. All right. I'll be over in a few minutes."

She stopped only long enough to put on sneakers. Her shorts and T-shirt were hardly suitable city attire, but then she wasn't going out on the town. She was going out to find Luc.

On the way over in the cab, it occurred to her that she might be going straight into trouble. If Luc had a woman with him . . .

The security guard gave her his key. It clanked loudly against the big blue plastic disk as she stepped into the elevator. The sound made her nerves tighten and skitter inside, like moths beating against a windowpane.

At Luc's door she rang the buzzer. Again. And again. No answer. At last, her heart hammering, she opened the door, turned on the light, walked inside, and closed it behind her.

She went hesitantly down the short hall, her anxiety and trepidation mingled together in a heart-stopping combination. She forced herself to step out into the living room. And there he was, sprawled on the couch, his head twisted to one side, one leg rolled off the edge of the cushion, his booted heel balancing on the floor.

He slept quietly, buzzing little breaths going in and out of his mouth. His chin was dark with beard and his well-groomed hair was mussed and he was wearing the same clothes she had last seen him in, only now they had a very definite well-worn look . . . and an aroma to match. The empty bottle told her exactly how he had spent the rest of that night—and all of today.

"Oh, Luc." She went to him and knelt beside him to lay her head on his chest, assuring herself that he really was warm and alive. "Luc. I didn't want to hurt you."

He slept on, unaware.

She got to her feet, knowing she would have to go back down with the security guard's key and tell him that she had found Luc and that he was all right. She did that and returned to

Luc's apartment, closing and locking the door from the inside. Then she went to the phone to call Karin.

"That's not like Luc," Karin said bluntly, when Rana told her what had happened. "Do you want me to come over and sit with you or something?"

"No, that isn't necessary. I'll . . ." she hesitated and then said briskly, "I'll stay with him tonight and call you in the morning."

"Are you sure he's all right?"

"Quite sure. Don't worry. He'll have some headache tomorrow, but other than that, he'll live."

CHAPTER SIX

She tried to get the boot off that dangling foot. She tugged and yanked, but the leather fit around his ankle like a glove. In one last exasperated effort, she pulled with all her might. The boot came free—but somehow Luc slid to the floor, rear first, his head flopping back against the cushion.

"Oh, no—"

"What the hell," he mumbled, rousing briefly. In the next instant his head had sagged to the floor. He stretched out full length and was snoozing again.

Her fear vanished, to be replaced by a strong surge of anger. She said a very succinct word under her breath, pulled off his other boot easily now that his shoulder was more or less braced against the front of the couch, and began to unbutton his shirt. He opened bleary, unseeing eyes. "Wha's going on?"

"Something's coming off," she said crisply. "Your shirt." She wrinkled her nose. "To put it bluntly, Luc Garrett, you need a bath."

He stared at her glassily. "Bath?" he asked, as if he had never heard the word before.

"Bath," she repeated firmly, feeling like Nurse Nora. "You smell like one of your horses."

He sniffed and considered it. "Insult to the horses," he mumbled.

"Probably." As she bent over him, her fingers going to the buttons of his shirt, he gave her the sly, considering look of a man whose faculty for reasoning was almost completely gone. Then he closed one eye in a stage wink and threw a heavy arm over her shoulder. "You're kinda cute. Are you new in the neighborhood?"

"Don't ply me with your silver-tongued flattery, Garrett," she shot back, her heart clamoring with a new ache. "I'm immune to your wiles . . . especially when you smell like a gin factory."

"Sc—otch," he got out with a great deal of difficulty. "It was scotch. Gotta get your facts right, Ms. O'Neill, fellow writer, fellow observer of human nature, fellow—" He stopped and peered at her, those vacant blue eyes roaming over her T-shirt. "Not a fellow," he murmured. "Definitely not a fellow," and closed his eyes again.

She gritted her teeth and went on undressing him. The crisp linen shirt that she had admired on him the night before was sodden and clinging to his skin. He felt clammy in the air-conditioned atmosphere of the apartment. She had to get his soaked clothes off and find something else for him to wear, a robe maybe. She finished unbuttoning his shirt. "Lift up," she said to him, her hand under his nape.

"Wha' you doing now? Undressing me?" The blue eyes made a valiant effort to focus. "My fondesh dream, having you undress me."

She half-suspected him of trying to disconcert her on purpose. Yet he was hardly in any condition to be thinking clearly. That bottle was empty. Had it been full when he started? Perhaps she should call a doctor.

Because she was worried and disturbed and had no outlet for her churning emotions, she said sharply, "Luc, I want you to get up and take a shower or I'm going to call a doctor."

Luc opened his eyes and gave her the blank stare she was beginning to know and hate. "What are you going to call him?"

She groaned, her exasperation spiraling. "Probably expensive, which is what he'll be if he gets dragged out here to see you on a house call and finds out there's nothing more seriously wrong with you than a pickled brain."

With great dignity he said, "My brain is not pickled. It's just slightly numb. I was applying an anes—anes—thetic."

"Well, you'll be pleased to know it took. Sit up, cowboy."

He amazed her by obeying, pulling her toward him to steady himself and saying in a formal, didactic voice, "I don't like your tone, lady. The word cowboy should be used with the proper respect."

"Sorry." She wasn't.

"It's an old and honorable term first used to label the loyalist guerrillas in the Revoloosh—Reveoloosh—"

"Revolutionary War?" she supplied helpfully.

"Yeah, that."

She stared at him. How could he still be thinking like a writer when he had had so much to drink? She said, "I have no doubt that you were one of those guerrillas in a past life, my friend."

The sober writer disappeared. He gave her another of those lecherous winks. "Bein' a gorilla isn't so bad. Wanna join me in some monkey business?"

She ordered her mouth in line to keep from smiling. She didn't dare encourage him. He was more wide-awake now than he had been, but she wasn't sure whether that was good or bad. Good for Luc, perhaps. Bad for her. She held him, propping up his upper body against the front of the couch. "Can you stand up?"

"Is this a test?" He smiled up at her, his face full of bad boy charm. She knelt beside him and got her feet under her to get some leverage so that she could lift him with her arm around his waist. He tossed an arm over her shoulder and the tips of his fingers brushed her breast. The sharp, leaping reaction of her body made her say, "On your feet, Garrett, or I'm going to call that doctor and leave you with a bill that will shock you into instant sobriety."

Pushing, shoving, cajoling, with more sheer brute strength than grace, she got him to his feet. With his arm still over her shoulder and his body leaning heavily against hers, she guided him in a lopsided turn that left Ginger Rogers and Fred Astaire's reputation unchallenged, and headed down the hall, praying that his room was that door on the left, praying that she had guessed right and that there was a private bathroom off the bedroom.

There was; it was a tiled sultan's delight with salmon walls and a swirling black and white marble floor. She looked at the pattern and thought it would be a good thing never to be sick and come into this room. She propped Luc up against the counter of the long vanity.

"I'm going to have to undress you, Garrett," she mumbled to him, and then in a heartfelt tone, "and believe me, this is going to hurt me more than it does you."

He looked at her with glazed interest, as if some remnant of sanity whispered that if he kept his eyes focused in her direction long enough he could actually see her.

"You're a very interesting lady, have I ever told you that?"

"Not recently." She clenched her teeth together and inserted her fingers in the buckle of his belt. If he turned charming while she was undressing him, she'd strangle him.

He laid a casual hand between her breasts. "You have such interesting topography. Much more interesting than mine."

She plucked his hand away from her body and put it firmly back on the counter. Of their own accord, her eyes flickered over his tanned chest, muscular, but not overly so, the curling hairs of brown covering him just enough to invite a woman's fingers to explore. Interesting topography definitely depended on your point of view. She wished Luc's was not quite so—appealing.

"You may have a reputation for accuracy," she muttered, "but you don't always know what you're talking about."

He didn't seem to hear her. "You have a way with brown hair," he said, his hand cupping her head. "What do you do to it to make it so—touchable?"

"Wash it daily." The snap of his jeans came free. Now all she had to do was run the zipper down. She took hold of the metal tab—and groaned inwardly. She shouldn't have tried this at all.

110

She should have let him sleep. She had no business undressing Luc Garrett and putting him in the shower. Yet suppose the situation were reversed. Suppose it was she who needed care. She knew Luc wouldn't have hesitated. He would have attended to her needs briskly and thoroughly and had her in bed before she knew it.

She braced herself . . . and pulled. The black denims clung. She had to ease them down over his long, well-shaped thighs and—a word escaped her. He was wearing one of the newer types of underwear, a low-cut, black bikini, and it fit him to perfection.

Quickly, she pulled his pants down and focused on his feet. Oh, no. She'd forgotten to take off his socks.

"Hang on to the counter, Garrett," she instructed him tersely, intensely aware of those long, muscular legs just above her as she lifted his foot to divest him of both sock and pant leg.

They went through the same procedure for the other leg, and when the black denims were lying in a heap on the floor, slowly, reluctantly, she rose.

"Luc . . . I can't . . . would you take off your—"

"Wha's the matter?" He gave her that earnest stare.

"Nothing," she said coolly. "You'll just have to wear your— the rest of your clothes in the shower and pretend it's a bathing suit." She would deal with getting those bikinis off later.

One palm against his chest to steady him, she said, "Stand there, Luc. Don't move. I'm going to turn on the shower for you."

He smiled.

Carefully, easing away from him with her arm still stretched toward him so that she could catch him if he suddenly fell forward, she stepped toward the shower stall and turned on the water. After a cautious glance at him that assured her he hadn't moved, she adjusted the water temperature and came back to him. "Okay now. In you go."

They resumed their position, she butted up under his shoulder, Luc's arm thrown heavily over her. At the shower door, she said, "Luc, let go of me."

"Come in with me. Take a shower with me."

"Luc, I have my clothes on—" He pushed her into the shower ahead of him and stepped inside and closed the door. She gasped in surprise and shock as the warm water hit her.

"Soap," he said with a satisfied sound. "Gotta use soap."

He took up the bar and ran it over her T-shirted back with the sober concentration of the very inebriated.

"Luc, you're crazy, Luc . . ." In spite of herself, she felt laughter bubbling up from deep inside her. She was soaked to the skin, and it was too late to worry about it.

Luc stopped massaging the soap over her back and looked at her with a comic concern. "Wha's the matter?"

Laughing, choking, she collapsed forward, rested her arms on his shoulders, and bowed her head to let the spasms of helpless laughter come out and not drown herself in the process. Her clothes sticking to every inch of her, she stood inches away from the almost naked body of Luc Garrett and shook with mirth.

"Rana, wha's the matter?" He lifted a hand to her hair in the gentlest of gestures.

"Nothing," she said, feeling him lift a sodden strand of hair away from her face as she looked up into the beautifully sculptured contours of his. "Not a thing is wrong." Water poured over her like a waterfall, misting her vision, beading Luc's brown hair with diamonds. "Everything's just fine"—knowing that never again would she wonder if it was possible to fall deeply in love with one special man in a microsecond.

He looked at her as if he thought she had suddenly lost her mind. With that puzzled frown still pulling his dark brows together, he shifted his grip and began to rub the soap over her shoulders and then carefully, down over her breasts, not seeming to notice the friction her T-shirt caused or the flesh that sprang to life under his hands.

"Luc—"

112

He knelt, and her hips and thighs got the same treatment, a no-nonsense scrubbing that obliterated that brief flare of sexual desire. Soapy water coursed down her legs to puddle in her sneakers. She felt as sodden as a puppy left out in the rain—and as defenseless.

"Luc, that's enough. Luc, I'm"—his earnest efforts to act as her bath slave and his tickling touch on her backside brought more laughter—"clean now."

He straightened, lurching against her. He pulled back immediately, as if he were afraid he might have hurt her.

"You use the soap on yourself," she told him, more to distract his attention from her than anything else. She was too light-headed with love and laughter to do anything but lean back against the wall in helpless surrender and let the water pour over her soapy clothes.

He shook his head and handed her the soap. "No. You do me."

He waited, the destruction of his inhibitions by alcohol leaving him with a face that was totally open—and totally vulnerable. She couldn't refuse.

She took the bar and rubbed him with it, letting it slide over the curly-crisp hairs on his chest, steeling herself to receive the pulses of sensual pleasure from her fingertips. She made slow circles over his chest and his shoulders, watching him as her fingers moved in an imitation of a lover's caress. He was quiet, his eyes never leaving her face, but they were as glazed and unseeing as they had ever been. He had turned his attention inward, as if he were listening to music playing inside his head. She wondered if he really knew what was happening and if he would remember. He was almost like a great cat snuggling into the hand that caressed him, his body absorbed in sensuous enjoyment.

Facing him and hugging him like a teddy bear, she slid her cleansing massage around his ribs to his back. He moved closer, his hands coming up. She tensed, but he merely flattened his palms against the shower wall on each side of her to support

113

himself. She was relieved that he hadn't grabbed for her—until she realized that she was in a prison, a prison bounded on every side by Luc.

She bent her knees and slithered downward, her back to the wall, thankful to escape that trap of his arms—only to be faced with the attraction of thighs developed to rock hardness on the back of a horse, and legs curved with muscle. Quickly, efficiently, she soaped them and stood up inside his arms again.

His eyes searched her face in puzzled confusion. "Where did you go?"

She smiled. "Out for lunch. Did you miss me?"

"I thought you were gone," he whispered. Their eyes met. Luc's had lost their fuzzy look. They were dark and intent. The only sound in the shower was the sizzle of water. "Turn around and rinse yourself off," she told him huskily.

He dipped his head toward her. She braced herself for the kiss she knew was coming, her palms on his bare, soap-slicked chest, her heart doing hopscotch.

It was a strange, butterfly-light kiss . . . and over too soon.

He said in a drugged tone, "I know this is a dream—and I'm going to feel like hell when I wake up. But I . . ." he leaned forward and touched her lips lightly again with his in a tentative way that tore her heart from her body.

"Luc," she said when he lifted his head, "turn around. The soap is drying on your body."

"Will you go away again?"

"No," she said. "I won't go away again."

"Promise?"

He was like a small boy. "I promise, Luc. Now please. . . ." She took hold of his shoulder and gave him a little push in the direction she wanted him to go. Dutifully, he revolved slowly under the water.

"Time to get out," she said in a bright, commanding tone she remembered from watching old reruns of *Father Knows Best*. "You've been in here long enough. You'll catch cold in your wet . . . bathing suit."

She made the mistake of glancing down at him. The soft cotton was soaked and clinging.

The toes inside her soggy sneakers curled, and she felt suddenly very, very warm. "Open the door, Luc. It's like a Turkish bath in here."

Again, he obeyed her and stepped out into the steamy bathroom. She followed and ripped a towel out of the ring holder to throw over his shoulders, knowing she was only putting off the inevitable. She couldn't expect to get him dry with those wet bikinis sending rivulets of water coursing down through the hair-covered thighs.

She had to take them off him. She cursed herself for a fool. His underpants would have been much easier to take off a few minutes ago when they were dry.

She closed her eyes and slid her fingers between that hard hipbone and the soaked material. In one desperate yank, she stripped the clinging wet cotton away from his body and down over his legs. She got him to shift his weight, and then he was free of them. She tossed them away.

Without looking at him, she grabbed another towel and wrapped it around his hips, tucking a corner under at his waist. She turned and saw the white terry cloth robe hanging from the hook on the back of the door. She heaved a sigh of relief and took it down. Somehow, she managed to get him to poke his arms into the sleeve holes.

As she tied the belt around his lean waist and slipped the towel underneath it away, he touched her lightly, his fingers playing over the shoulder seam of her damp T-shirt. "You're all wet."

"Surprise, surprise," she muttered in an ironic tone, toweling his legs and feet briskly. "Lean against the counter while I take off my sneakers."

She kicked off her shoes and wrapped a towel around herself to keep the water from running down on the thick shag carpeting in Luc's bedroom. Taking him by the arm, she guided him out of the doorway and pressed him toward the bed.

At the side of the bed she held him at bay with one hand and pulled the covers back with the other.

"Get in, Luc."

He climbed in obediently. She thanked God he was so tractable. If he hadn't been, she would never have been able to handle that rangy six foot two frame with its muscled underpinning.

"You come with me," he said, grabbing her and pulling her toward him, every bit of that wonderful tractability disappearing like smoke.

Off guard, she hadn't been braced for his sudden possession of her wrist. "No, Luc, I can't. I've got to get out of these wet clothes."

He was like a stubborn child. "Can't let you go," he mumbled, his fingers tightening, his eyes closed. "Can't let go of a dream. Once you let go of a dream, you never get it back again."

"Luc, listen to me—you need to sleep. I'll be right here."

"Want you," he said, opening his eyes to stare at her in confusion. "Want you with me." Louder, the edge of desperation giving his voice a throaty rasp, "Need you."

And there it was again. Another opportunity to hurt him, rising out of nowhere to stare her in the face and haunt her.

Yet if he thought he was dreaming—would she really be hurting him if she walked away?

"Luc, please . . ."

His eyes were closed, and his head was back against the pillows, but the grip on her wrist shackled her to him. "Need you," he repeated in a weary tone.

Torn, she stood looking down at him, seeing the mussed dark hair, the mouth that had touched hers so gently, the frown that still lingered on his brow. She didn't want to give in to him— and she didn't have the strength to walk away. And was he asking for so much really? She could lie down beside him for a little while, and after he fell asleep, she could put on her damp clothes and go home. When Luc woke in the morning, he would

116

never know for sure if she had really been there—or if he had dreamed it all.

"Luc, please. You have to let go of me. I can't lie down beside you with these wet clothes on. I have to change."

He opened his eyes. "Are you going to stay?"

"Yes," she said, "but you have to let me go find something dry to wear."

"You'll come back?"

The anxious rasp made her want to weep. "Yes, Luc. I'll come back."

His grip slackened. "Hurry." He smiled a sleepy half smile, those black lashes long against his cheek. "I'll wait right here."

In his closet, pushed back away from the bulk of Luc's clothes, she found a silvery gray dress robe made of some expensive fabric that felt like rain water on her skin. The robe must have belonged to Luc's landlord. She stripped off her wet clothes, put the robe on, and draped her things over the vanity in the bathroom to dry. She picked up the wet towels and put them in the hamper. She towel-dried her hair. And then, when there was nothing more left to do, she went back into the bedroom and slid into the bed beside him.

He opened his arms to her immediately. "Rana," he breathed in a contented sigh, and when she snuggled her head into the niche in his shoulder and stretched out against his warm, deliciously male body swathed in terry cloth, she closed her eyes. And strangely enough, she relaxed. Immediately, his breathing slowed and shifted to a deep rhythm that told her he was asleep. She would only stay a little while longer, until she was sure she wouldn't wake him when she moved, and then she would get up. . . .

She couldn't move. She was crushed, trapped. She brought up her hand to fend off the dark prison that closed in around her and felt the back of her hand connect with Luc's forehead.

A deep rasp said in her ear, "Oh, my God. My head."

No wonder she'd felt imprisoned. Luc lay on his side, one

sinewy leg thrown over both of hers, his arm heavy on her abdomen. She came wide-awake, suddenly aware that it was morning and she had spent the night in his arms. Her heart pounding, she twisted to look up into his face.

Luc swore with the same succinct skill he might have used on a herd of cows. "For God's sake, don't shake the bed like that."

She had barely moved. "I'm sorry," she said. His blue eyes were slowly, painfully coming open.

"You should be. I—" Recognition dawned. "Rana!"

She wanted to hit him right on the top of his aching head. Luc was not surprised to wake up with a woman in his bed— but he *was* surprised to wake up with her in his bed. The warm flickers of desire died an instant death. She said dryly, "You were expecting Doctor Livingstone?"

"What the hell are you doing here?"

She gave him a look that would have frozen fire. "I'm wondering that same thing."

"I can't remember," he said, rubbing a lean finger over his temple. "I remember coming home, getting a bottle, but I don't remember you—"

"Very flattering, Garrett."

He lifted his head to look at her, groaned, and put his hand to his forehead. "Oh, my God, my head feels like dried buffalo meat."

"How literate of you." She was so angry that she ached. She wondered why she'd been such a fool and how in the name of heaven she was going to get out of bed when the darn robe had come open and Luc was lying on half of it.

He looked down at her, his hand on his head. "We didn't—"

"No, we didn't," she said, her voice cold with fury. "Your virtue is quite intact."

The pained look in his eyes gave way to something that might have been amusement. "Is that why you're so angry?"

"I'm angry because I didn't expect to be here when you woke up. I'm angry because I was stupid enough to let a drunken cowboy sweet-talk me into getting into bed with him."

He leaned back, half closing his eyes, whether in speculation or pain, she couldn't tell and said fervently, "I wish I could remember how I did it."

That made her angrier than ever. "Well, I do remember," she shot back, every word clipped, "and believe me, it won't work twice."

"But, as you said, nothing happened."

"No, thank goodness. Now, move, so I can get out of bed."

"Why do I have to move—" He reached out. Below the sheet his hand connected with a bare, silky thigh.

She jumped as if he'd hit her. "Don't touch me."

She was as friendly as a spitting cat. Then why in hell was she in bed with him? Oh, God, if he could only think. His head felt like the inside of a slot machine right after a big win, everything going out, nothing coming in.

She lay beside him, seething. "Are you going to move?"

"You don't know what you're asking," he said in a muffled tone.

"What a fraud you are, Garrett. I thought all cowboys could spend a night with a bottle and a woman and wake up the next morning ready for more."

"Down on two counts," he murmured. "Care to try for number three?"

"Get off my robe."

He lifted his head, winced, propped it into one hand with his elbow in the pillow, and focused his gaze on her. "Your robe?" his voice mocked softly. "That looks like Kensington's robe."

"I should have known this thing would belong to a man named Kensington. Will you move, Garrett?"

His eyes roved over her body under the sheet. "Somehow I don't think Kensington ever filled it out quite like that."

"Get up."

"I don't think so—not till you tell me what I did to make you so angry."

Through clenched teeth, she said, "I'm not angry."

"Of course you're not."

"Stop playing games, Garrett, and get off the robe."

He closed his eyes. "Please, not so loud."

In a soft, lethal tone, she said, "Let me up."

"I don't think so. Not till I've explored all the possibilities of this curious situation. . . ."

He lowered his head, then stopped and grimaced at the pain.

"You can't," she said, in a sudden, panicky self-defense against the pounding warmth in her chest where his hair-rough skin pressed against her breasts. "You have a headache."

"I'll take some aspirin," he murmured and found her mouth.

She resisted. He wooed her with love nibbles, coaxing her to give in, urging her to respond. He teased her, tugging at her lips with his teeth, willing her to open them to him. Then, as their mouths and bodies touched, the playfulness vanished and passion flowered, warm and engulfing.

"Luc. Oh, Luc . . ."

"Rana. Let me—" he swooped, thrusting his tongue into her mouth, claiming her with a sweet possessiveness that melted her anger and sent her temperature soaring.

Still kissing her, gently, very gently, he drew back the sheet. His hands flowed over the silken robe and pushed it aside to discover a satiny strip of her. Her body responded, her senses focusing sharply on those warm, wonderful hands. He leaned over to taste her breast—and a moan of pain escaped him. She clasped both sides of his head and lifted him into her vision. "Luc, you're in no condition for this."

"Are you?" he said softly, and she knew at once what he meant. He was asking if she was protected.

At the look of pain that crossed her face, he said throatily, "Rana, I want you. Beautiful lady, I've wanted you for so long. I can't just kiss you and let you go. You know that, don't you?"

"I'm not protected, Luc."

His eyes darkened.

She made a move to roll away from him. "I knew you wouldn't want to take the risk. . . ."

He stopped her with a hard hand clamped around her waist.

"Risk be damned. It's you I was thinking about. You don't want to make a commitment, but believe me, having my baby would sure as hell be a commitment to me."

She lay still and quiet under his eyes. His hand tightened on her hip. "Let me take the responsibility."

He waited, watching her.

Tortured, she stared up into his haggard face that was dark with beard. "I still don't think—"

He destroyed her defenses simply by laying his hand on the exposed curve of her breast, very gently stroking the hardening bud through the silk robe. His other hand whisper-caressed her face as if she were a child he was quieting. She felt as if she were drowning, a glutton at a feast of sensual pleasure.

"I'll only take whatever you give me," he said huskily, leaning over her to kiss her. "But if you intend to walk away from me, woman, do it now."

"I'm not going anywhere, Luc," she said huskily.

He kissed her, a long, hard kiss that claimed and exulted. "I'm going to get the aspirin and the other—essentials. Don't go away. Promise me you won't go away."

"I won't."

He pressed his fingers against his forehead and rolled away from her to get out on the other side of the bed.

Two steps out of bed, he said, "My God. My head is pounding like crazy. . . ."

Rana pulled the sheet up over her. "It's the door, Luc. Someone's at the door."

He grimaced. "I don't believe it. Ignore it. Maybe they'll go away."

A deep male voice bellowed. "Luc Garrett. Open up, you son of a snake, or I'll break this door down."

Luc groaned.

Rana said, "Who is it?"

"My brother. I use him as the prototype for all the villains in my books. What in the hell has got into him? He sounds as if he was at the front of a longhorn stampede."

121

"You'd better answer the door."

With a resigned sigh, he tied his belt. "I'll try and get rid of him as soon as I can."

"Luc! Open this damn door."

Luc went out. Rana huddled under the covers, wondering what was wrong with Luc's brother. . . .

"Hello, Conrad."

There was a sound like a dull thud, and then moaning, and the angry voice saying, "Why can't you stand still and fight like a man? Where is she? She said she was coming here; now where is she? She sure as hell isn't sleeping on the couch."

Luc, confused, said simply, "Who?"

"Who?" Rana heard the rage in a voice that had a deep rasp very like Luc's. "Who? The crazy young female who came chasing to New York to be with you, that's who."

"I don't know any crazy young female," Luc said with impeccable logic, and Rana was almost sure from the tone he used that he was holding his head.

There was silence, then a door, from the sound of it, the one across the hall, crashed against a wall. Luc's protest came an instant later. "My God, man, could you make a little less noise? You're enough to wake up the dead."

"That's what you're going to be if I don't find her soon. And she sure as hell better not be in your bedroom. Is she in your bedroom, Luc?" The voice had dropped to a low, lethal tone.

Rana got up, pulled the robe around her, ran a hand through her hair to muss it more than it was already, and went to the door. Opening it, she leaned against it and poked a knee out from under her robe in her best Mae West imitation and said, "Luc, what is all the racket about out here?"

Conrad Garrett was two inches away from her, and she almost lost her nerve when he whirled on her. He was younger and taller than his brother and boiling with fury. But Rana had the satisfaction of seeing him gaze at her in stupefied surprise, his eyes going over the silky robe and registering the fact that she had little or nothing on underneath.

"You're not Karin," he said, still not fully accepting her presence in Luc's apartment.

"Is that a point in my favor or against it?" She perused his tall frame clad in jeans and a blue plaid shirt with a casual thoroughness that kept him at bay.

Conrad Garrett absorbed her cool annoyance with an astonishment that deflated his anger. "I . . ." He was clearly at a loss for words.

"Well, now that we've got that settled, would you mind taking your loud voice and your wild accusations and getting out of here?"

She saw Luc lifting his head to gaze at her in surprise. He was propped up against the wall, where, unless she missed her guess, Conrad had taken a crack at him . . . and missed.

He looked at Luc. "I need to know where Karin is."

"Why didn't you say so?" Rana said smoothly. "She's staying with Clem and Helen Davis. Just a minute. I'll write down the address. Luc, darling, paper and pen?"

His face revealing nothing, he indicated a desk on the wall to her left. She went over to it and bent to open a drawer, the opening of her robe exposing a long, slim length of leg. She heard Conrad make a sound, a swallowed gulp. Calmly, as if she hadn't heard a thing, she wrote for a moment and then handed him the piece of paper.

"You know Karin?" Luc's brother looked strange—off-balance. She guessed that didn't happen to Conrad Garrett very often in his life.

"I had lunch with her yesterday." Was it only yesterday? "She speaks very highly of you, but I must say, I can't see that it's justified. Perhaps love is blind, after all."

"Love?" He looked shell-shocked.

"Well, of course. And you must love her, too, since you were ready to murder your brother on the mere chance that she *might* be here with him." She smiled at him. "Hadn't you better be going?"

Conrad moved woodenly toward the door. When he was

gone, Luc said, "I did enjoy that. Especially the Mae West part."

"I did it for Karin," she said coolly. "I like her."

"Everybody likes Karin," Luc said, moving carefully around the couch toward her. "And very few people get the best of my brother—myself included."

"I didn't want to—intimidate him. I merely wanted to get him out of here before he did you bodily harm. You're not in the best condition right at the moment."

He took her in his arms. "I'm improving minute by minute. All I need is the healing touch of Doctor Livingstone." His mouth lingered near her ear. "You did say that was your name, didn't you?" He bent his head and found the tender spot in the hollow of her throat.

His clean, musky smell tantalized her. Pushing the edge of the robe aside, his lips moved lower. "Luc, I . . . I can't. I'm sorry. I am going to get dressed and . . . go."

He lifted her head and stared down at her. "I am going to kill my brother," he said softly, "in the slowest, most painful way possible."

"It isn't his fault."

"Oh yes, it is. If it weren't for him, we'd be making love right now."

"Well, we aren't. So—"

"That's a temporary aberration that can easily be fixed."

"No, Luc. It's not the best of times. You're hung over and I'm—"

"—not hung over enough."

She lifted a shoulder. "If that's what you want to think—go ahead. It isn't the first time I've been accused of being inhibited."

She moved toward the bedroom.

From behind her he said in a peculiar, terse tone, "If I promise not to touch you . . . will you stay?"

She turned slowly, the strained note in his voice catching her

124

as nothing else could have. It was very like the way he had asked her to stay with him last night.

"Stay?"

"For breakfast. For lunch. For dinner." A smile lifted his lips. "We'll have spaghetti."

She looked at him, her gray eyes steady. She wanted to stay; she ached to stay. But Luc was lucid and on his feet. He no longer needed her. And if she stayed—she would end up in his arms. She wanted to be there now. She could hardly bear to see him standing there across the room in that terry robe and not go to him and touch him. Last night had broken down all the barriers.

"I really think I'd better go." She turned away before he could say anything and went into the bedroom. In the bathroom, behind the closed door, she slipped into her cool, damp clothing.

Feeling numb, she walked back out into the front room. Luc hadn't moved. His eyes followed her as she walked toward him.

In front of him, she stopped. "Don't forget to take that aspirin," she whispered and went past him to the door.

As she opened it, he said in a rasp of pain, "I swore I'd never use force to hold you. But one day—one day, Rana O'Neill, you'll come to me—of your own free will. And you won't go away."

He stood there, hard and male, his face dark with beard, the wall behind him an elegant gold-and-silver-striped silk. She shook her head, her throat feeling as if she were trying to swallow a stone. "Good-bye, Luc," she said quickly and went out, closing the door behind her.

CHAPTER SEVEN

That evening, around ten o'clock, while she sat at the computer and put the finishing touches on her column, the doorbell rang.

It was Luc, a sober, correct Luc in a heather-blue western suit with blue suede insets at the shoulders, a glittery string tie, and his brown hair combed to an unusual state of neatness. He looked as if he were on his way out to an evening on the town.

"May I come in?"

He was so cool and detached that to refuse his request would have made her seem foolish. "Yes, of course."

She looked around at the barren living room and hated it suddenly. "Why don't you come out to the kitchen? I was just going to stop and fix myself some coffee." She hesitated, her eyes going over his male elegance, his smooth cheeks. He looked very different from the last time she had seen him. "Do you have time for a cup?"

"Yes, thank you," he said with such a grave politeness that she could hardly believe he was the same man who had been so inebriated that he had dragged her, fully clothed, into the shower the night before.

She walked ahead of him into the kitchen and gestured toward the brightly polished snack bar. "Sit down. The coffee will be ready in a minute."

She did all the necessary things with her usual ease, tipped the filter with the old grounds into the garbage, put in a fresh filter, filled it with coffee and poured the water through, but she was wearing a pair of brief shorts and an old, tight-fitting cotton shirt she should have thrown away ages ago, and judging from

Luc's quietness, and the live-wire tautness of her nerves, for all his apparent detachment, Luc was watching every move she made.

Not looking at him, she slid into the chair across from him . . . and then lifted her eyes to his.

He said, "I came to tell you that Conrad is taking Karin home tomorrow. And . . . they're getting married at Christmastime."

Rana's smile was spontaneous. "I'm glad."

Luc didn't answer her smile. In that same cool tone he said, "Karin wanted me to invite you to the wedding."

"That's very kind of her." Rana's cheeks warmed with pleasure despite Luc's evident lack of enthusiasm at delivering the message.

"Haven't you forgotten something?"

Luc's brilliant blue gaze was too piercing. She got up and went to get the spoons and napkins. "What did I forget?"

"That's very kind of her—but."

She stood at the counter, facing him. "I'm sure she doesn't really expect me to come."

"Of course she does. You were kind enough to take her to lunch when you met under less than . . . ideal circumstances. And a woman from Wyoming doesn't forget a kindness—nor does she extend insincere invitations."

She toyed with a spoon and cast about for a less dangerous topic. "Does it get cold in Wyoming in December?"

"Depends on where you are. If you're up in the mountains, you'll sure as heck get cold. Wintertime temperatures can range from twenty degrees below zero to fifty below."

"Is the Hughes ranch up in the mountains?"

"Yes. But they have a house closer to town on the lower elevations that they use in the wintertime. Karin wants to be married there."

"She's very lucky."

He closed his mind to the wistful tone in her voice. He couldn't feel sorry for her. Not now. Because if he did—he

128

wouldn't be able to walk away. This whole thing was a damn fool idea, and he knew it. He should never have allowed Karin to talk him into it. He didn't even know what had happened last night, although something had teased at the back of his mind when he'd showered this morning. . . . He schooled himself to keep to the subject at hand. "I'm meeting Karin and Con in a few minutes. At least let me tell them you're thinking about coming."

"I . . . can't promise that." The aroma of hot coffee filled the kitchen. When it was ready, Rana poured out a cup for Luc and a cup for herself. So he was going out with Con and Karin for the evening. Had he invited another woman along to make the party a foursome?

"Do you use cream or sugar?"

He shook his head.

"No, of course, you don't," she said, smiling faintly, concentrating desperately to think of something to say to take her mind off the thought of Luc with another woman. "A cowboy's coffee has to be strong enough to float a horseshoe."

"That's an exaggerated story. We test our coffee with something much lighter. A piece of barbed wire." He said it soberly enough, but his eyes held a small glimmer of amusement.

"Are you sure you don't test your barbed wire with your coffee? If the barb melts, you buy a better grade of wire the next time?"

"I don't think we've ever tried that. But it doesn't sound like a bad idea." He drank a bit and set his cup down. "Have you finished your column for today?"

"Pretty much. I was just putting on the finishing touches."

"Actually," he said in a strange, diffident tone, "I'm here because . . . Karin wants you to go out with us and help her and Con celebrate their engagement this evening."

An evening. An entire evening with Luc, watching him from across a table, brushing against his arm, perhaps even dancing with him. And at the end of that evening, after hours of seeing him and watching him smile and feeling her body come to stinging life at the merest accidental touch of his hand, she would be so hungry for him that her will to resist him would be gone.

"I can't, Luc. I . . . still have quite a bit to do and—"

"I told Karin you wouldn't. But she insisted I ask. She has this harebrained idea that you . . . care for me."

Silvery eyes eloquent, she stared at him in silent anguish. "And so you thought you'd humor me by asking me out?"

"No," he said in a tight voice, "I was humoring myself." Before she could reply, he made a sound and slid off the stool. "I'd better be going." He turned his back on her and walked out of the kitchen. She sat for a moment, trying to calm her racing heart and then went out after him.

He stood in the middle of that barren living room, his head turning slowly around, taking in the carpet-covered cubes and the pillows.

"I heard once that your mother became a recluse after your father died. For those few weeks she was alive after his death, she refused to let anyone touch a thing in the house. She kept everything exactly the way it was the day he walked out for the last time." He swung back to look at her. "Is that why this place looks like the inside of an abstract painting?"

Through a mist of pain, she whispered, "Yes."

He nodded as if he had known the answer all along and she had only confirmed it. He said, "This suits you." Without warning he turned to her, clamped his hands around her waist, and lifted her straight up into the air.

"What are you doing? Put me down."

He swung her over a cube and stood her upright on it, steadying her until she regained her balance. He stepped away, as if he were surveying a sculpture he'd done. "This is where you belong. Now you're safe," he said in a strained tone, his dark face looking up at her. "Now you can't make any mistakes."

She couldn't move. She stared down at him, her body alive with shock.

"Comfortable up there on your pedestal, Rana?"

He turned his back to her and walked into the entryway. The door closed behind him. She stood there on top of the cube in her apartment and felt exactly like the statue he had made of her. Empty . . . and cold.

The moment he climbed into the cab with them, Karin plied him with questions. "Where is she? Is she getting ready? Will she meet us there?"

"She's not coming with us," he said bluntly and leaned forward to give the taxi driver the address of a small, intimate French place on Fifty-third Street that he was sure Karin would like and Con would hate. The thought gave him a small flicker of satisfaction.

"You mean she turned you down?" Karin sank back under Conrad's arm to rest against his shoulder, her smile gone.

"That's exactly what I mean."

"Why? What happened?" asked Karin.

"What happened?" He didn't look at Karin. He sat straight and faced the front, forcing his body to stillness. "Exactly what I told you would happen. She said no."

"To the wedding and everything?"

"Everything," he echoed in a hollow voice.

"But . . . didn't seeing you . . . dressed up and everything, didn't that move her?"

"To new heights," he said through gritted teeth with a bitter irony.

"But—"

Conrad heard the steely pain in his brother's voice. "Don't ask, honey. Better not to know."

Luc grimaced. For once, Conrad was showing consideration, as well he might, but it was a little damn late. Luc had had to restrain himself from strangling his brother when Con had come back with Karin an hour after the fiasco in Luc's apartment to apologize and tell him that he'd asked Karin to marry him. Luc had wanted to throw him against the wall, and Con

131

knew it. Con was treading very lightly now that he realized what he'd done . . . that somehow his untimely arrival had been a crucial turning point in Luc's relationship with Rana.

Luc told himself he couldn't let his black mood cast a pall on Con and Karin's evening. But when they entered the French country-style café, with its brick walls and antique mirrors, the first thing he had to do was tell the charming hostess that their reservation for a party of four was incorrect and that there would only be three dining at his table this evening. The lady's dark, large eyes were sympathetic. He could almost hear what she was thinking. Was monsieur such a clod that his lady friend had turned him down at the last minute? Yes, monsieur was. And the trouble was, monsieur didn't know exactly what kind of clod he had been. What had happened last night? The thought that he couldn't remember had driven him crazy all day. What in God's name had happened? Rana said they hadn't made love, and he believed that. He would have been in no condition for anything that—strenuous. But if they hadn't— why had she been in bed with him?

They were shown to a curved seat tucked behind a semicircle table. Luc stepped back to let the young lovers slide in next to each other. When they were settled, he sat down beside Karin and sprawled his long legs on the outside of the table.

A waiter came. Con and Karin ordered drinks; Luc asked for a glass of Perrier water. The thought of alcohol made him ill.

After their drinks were served, the waiter, a darkly handsome young man in a black suit as tight as a toreador's, smiled at Karin and recited the day's specialties, his eyes never leaving Karin's face for an instant. When they made their decisions and the waiter flashed another charming smile at Karin before he went away, Con muttered, "I wonder if he thinks 'mademoiselle' is responsible for zee tip."

Karin laughed up at him. "Are you jealous?"

"What do you think?"

"I can't understand why you should be. Just think how many years I've been in love with you."

"Well, let's see," Con drawled. "At your great age, it must be at least two."

Karin laid her hand over Con's and said in a light but serious tone, "I've loved you since I was seven. That's . . . thirteen and a half years."

As Luc watched, Conrad turned his hand and caught Karin's to bring her palm up to his mouth. "I've been a stupid a—"

"Umm," Karin interrupted quickly. "Not here, darling."

"Sorry."

Luc stared at his brother. Conrad Garrett, contrite and amiable, was a sight to see. A miracle achieved at the expense of his own happiness.

With her other hand, Karin reached out and touched Luc's arm. "Don't look so sad, Luc. I . . . want you to be happy."

"I am happy," he growled.

She cringed. "Of course." Deftly Karin changed the subject, telling them both about Helen and the volunteer work that she did for a children's hospital. "She's a wonderful woman. She cares for people, you know? She likes you a lot, Luc. She was sorry about that program on TV. She didn't realize anyone was taking a picture of you and Rana."

Luc's face turned to stone at the mention of Rana's name.

Karin apologized again and launched into an amusing anecdote about Helen and Clem together at the breakfast table, and the awkward moment passed. But after they had eaten and even Con had grudgingly agreed that the food was excellent, Karin leaned back against the leather-cushioned booth and said, "What you need, Luc, is a game plan."

"Game plan?" He wished he had ordered a drink. Perhaps another hangover was exactly the medicine he needed to counter Karin's optimistic chatter.

"Sure. A game plan to capture Rana. Isn't that the way things are done these days? Rana's not cooperating, right? Well, if a company decides to go in and buy another company, they devise a plan. If a country wants to take over another country, they plot the best way to go about it. What you need is a plot."

133

"Don't I always," he murmured dryly.

Luc's witticism sailed over Karin's head. "Let's see. What do we have to work with? Halloween is coming? Yes, that's it. You could haunt her."

Conrad said, "Haunt her? Honey, don't you think you're getting a little carried away?"

"Absolutely not. New York is a big city. If Rana won't go out with him, Luc could go for days without seeing her. He'll have to find other ways to see her . . . and make sure that she sees him." Karin looked at Luc, excitement making her eyes sparkle. "You have to be where she is. And you can't look—normal. You need something to make you stand out from the crowd, something to make her remember you when she walks away. Something that will stick in her mind. . . . Stick! That's it. Now listen, Luc . . ."

Karin outlined her plan, and when she finished, Luc shook his head. "Forget it. It's ridiculous."

With impeccable logic Karin said, "What have you got to lose?"

In the long, dismally bleak days that followed Luc's visit to her apartment, the most exciting thing that happened in Rana's life was the arrival of her chair. That weekend she experimented with placing it in different locations in the room . . . and decided that one piece of furniture looked slightly ridiculous with all the surrealistic cubes sitting around. She'd have to get rid of them. She was unable to do anything about it right away, though, because on Monday morning, as she worked frantically to beat a deadline, a freak surge of power put her computer out of commission. In a high state of panic she called Sam.

"What do you mean you can't transmit your column?" he barked at her over the phone.

"The thing doesn't work, that's what I mean. And it isn't going to work until I get somebody competent to look at it. I called a repairman, but he still isn't here."

"Get some hard copy off to us then. We'll put it out over the wire service."

She let out a breath. "You don't seem to understand, Sam. Without the computer I have no way to produce hard copy."

There was a long pause. Then Sam drawled in a dry voice, "There was an ancient invention I seem to remember. It was called a typewriter. Do you by any chance remember it?"

"Very funny."

"You wouldn't happen to have one, I suppose."

"I have an old Royal portable, sure. But the question mark key is broken, and the ribbon is as gray as sheets washed with brand B detergent. And I'm so used to the edit function of the computer that I'll make a million mistakes."

"Well, go buy some correction fluid," Sam barked. "And a ribbon. And write that damn column without asking any questions."

She absorbed Sam's two-edged directive and told him good-bye. After she hung up, she asked herself several questions. Why was she a writer? And why couldn't she stop missing Luc?

Missing him. She'd read a million words to describe the feeling, but none of them did justice to the great gaping hole inside her. When she got up in the morning he was there in her heart . . . but he wasn't there in reality. She could talk to him . . . but there was no rebuttal. She could see him . . . but he was like a hologram, a vision with no real substance . . . no will or mind of his own, only that which she gave him in her imagination. And she didn't want her own distorted version of him. She wanted him, the real Luc, who breathed and thought and answered her back and told her that he wanted and needed her.

One night she tossed restlessly in her bed, wanting desperately to get up, get dressed, and go to him. She held the thought at bay long enough, until, in her feverish state of need and loneliness, she dozed.

Words rose in her mind; images played in her brain. She was eighteen again and listening to that last bitter quarrel her parents had ever had. The quarrel that sent her father to his death.

Her mother's voice, cold, cutting. *You're such a pitiful case, John. You have a minor talent—enough to produce a few mediocre plays perhaps, but nothing more. You'll never be a Eugene O'Neill or even a Neil Simon, I'm afraid. You don't have enough creativity to become a great name. Your mind isn't free enough. You're too hidebound, too straightforward*—here her mother had paused and laughed a soft, mocking laugh—*too inhibited. You don't know how to let your mind fly.* . . .

You've told me that for years, her father had said wearily. *I think—I think I finally believe it.* Then he had gone out and tried to make his car fly. . . .

She closed her eyes against the pain. She had done the same thing to Luc. Not as viciously, perhaps, but she had set herself up as judge and jury. And it had happened almost without her noticing it. She had acted impulsively, out of her subconscious. And if she did it again . . . and again . . .

She had to stay away from him. For his sake, she had to.

The next day, her eyes great rings of tiredness, she went out and bought a large sectional couch. The purchase nearly wiped out her savings account, but after it was delivered, she sat in it as the afternoons went by, long, interminable afternoons followed by long, interminable evenings. She beat out columns on the old Royal portable, columns on pages stiff with correction fluid. Worse, her writing was just words, words that marched across the page and did nothing for her mind—or her heart. She wrote about the pulse of New York City; she wrote about the opening of a new musical on Broadway composed by a trio of talented young musicians; she wrote about a new book she had read on the way children learn which presented a theory of each person's wholeness with the universe. She didn't feel as if she were one with the universe. She felt separate, apart . . . and very, very lonely.

One warm day toward the end of September, she finished up her column and knew she had to get out of her apartment. She went to the coffee shop . . . and when she came out, she jumped in shock. Luc stood just across the street from her. He

136

leaned against the building, his face in the shadows. She couldn't see his eyes. The only thing she could see was the large grocery bag he held clasped in one arm—and the loaf of Italian bread in a white wrapper poking up out of the top.

The spaghetti dinner he had offered her.

She ran down the street in blind confusion, half-expecting him to come after her, more than half-praying that he would. He didn't.

She went to the dedication of a new government building that took place on the next Sunday afternoon. Luc was there—carrying the same grocery bag. She wanted to weep—or laugh, she wasn't sure which.

With combined exultation and dread, she began to watch for him. He disappeared. It was as if the earth had eaten him up. Then, when she had decided he'd given up his futile game of hide-and-seek, she came out of the Metropolitan Museum to find him standing there, that now-familiar bag in his arms. Panicked, she ran from him and inserted herself between a group of matrons from New Jersey and some school children from the Bronx. After she reached her apartment, it took two hours and a cold shower to quiet her rattling nerves.

She was reading some research material later that night when a knock sounded on her door.

She opened the door with shaking hands, her face bloodless.

"You're going flaky," Terry told her from the hallway, his eyes roving over her wan features with a wary concern.

She shook her head and stepped back to let him in, her throat tight. How could she deny his blunt words? He had said out loud what she was convinced had been happening during the last three weeks.

He'd come in to check out her latest furniture purchase, and now he sat with legs sprawled out in the center of the modular unit, his denim a contrast to the peacock-blue velvet. He looked around the room and then back at her. "How come you're buying all this furniture?"

She said the first thing that came into her mind. "I . . . needed it."

Terry gave her a I-don't-believe-it look. "You've needed furniture ever since you moved into this apartment. Why buy some now?"

"It's too complicated to explain."

"Which means you don't want to."

She made an attempt to pull herself together and tried to match his casual needling tone. "Don't I hear your mother calling you?"

Terry peered at her. "I don't know. Are you hearing strange voices?"

The flip replies began to come back to her, out of habit. They brought with them a wonderful feeling of normality. "Your mother doesn't have a strange voice."

He shrugged. "It's a little weird." He settled back into the cushions and studied her. "When's your stockbroker friend coming over to try out the new couch?" At her threatening look, he added hastily, "I mean to sit on it."

She felt drained, suddenly, not able to keep up the flow of bright answers. "I really don't know."

"Or what about that western dude? I haven't seen him around lately."

"I do seem to have this talent for misplacing men, don't I?"

He gave her a mock leer. "You have me."

"You just love me for my computer."

"Which, right now, is nonfunctioning," he said. "When are you going to get it fixed?"

"Soon, I hope."

He shrugged. "Oh, well, there's still your cookies." He gave her a covetous grin. "When are you going to bake some more?"

Vivid memory spilled through her. Luc, tasting the sugar—and her. She fought back the image. "Halloween's not too far away."

"Be real. It's still September."

"Patience, little boy."

He got to his feet, his eyes on hers. "You know something, O'Neill? You really do look lousy. Anything wrong?"

"Probably a cold coming on."

"You better take two aspirin and go to bed. It might be terminal."

"Thank you, doctor. You won't be offended if I get a second opinion?"

"Suit yourself." At the door, he gazed down at her. "Want me to tell Mom she should look at you?"

"Aren't you overdoing it a bit?"

"Your eyes look funny."

"They 'look' just fine. I can see perfectly well with them."

He shook his head. "Why do I try to word-fight with a writer? I should know better." At the door he turned. "Never mind the handshake. I don't want to get whatever you've got."

She doubted if loving Luc Garrett was contagious. "You won't. Good-bye, Terry."

He left and she closed the door behind him. The empty quiet echoed in her ears. She went to her typewriter and sat down to write—because she had to.

Two mornings later the words she had written were being delivered to a fourth of the doorsteps in New York, and Luc Garrett's was one of them. He opened the door, retrieved his paper, and went inside to read it. A cup of coffee sat on the low Queen Anne table. He dropped down on the velvet couch in the corner within reaching distance of his mug and spread the paper across his jeaned knee. He read her column slowly, carefully. It was a wonderful, readable discussion of an art exhibit done by a new artist. There were flashes of insight into what makes good art, and in stunning contrast, a vivid description of the way an elderly woman had held a heavy toddler in her arms for an entire hour as she walked around the gallery, just so the child could see each picture clearly.

Reading her column was a fine torture because it brought her close. He could almost see her talking animatedly about the show. He laid his head back on the couch and thought wearily of what lay ahead of him today. Autograph sessions at three New York bookstores. An interview with a news reporter over lunch, a man who would be sure to ask him about that television talk program where they'd shown that damnable photograph of Rana and him sprawled on the floor. A meeting with Patrice at 3:00 in her office to go over the proposal for his new book where he'd have to try and answer her probing questions that would no doubt bring to light all the weaknesses in the damn thing. Play rehearsal tonight. He had to be there because Jennifer Halding, the actress playing the lead female role, wanted a "very slight" change in the dialogue.

He let the paper fall away from his hands and thought about what he would do if he could spend the day exactly the way he wanted to spend it.

Buy two sandwiches and a bottle of wine and go to Rana's apartment. See her come to the door, watch her smile in surprise at the sight of him. Hear her express delighted, instant approval of his impromptu invitation. Feel the warmth of her fingers as he took her hand. Ride to Central Park with her in a taxi; watch her smooth slender legs lift and straighten as she climbed out of the car. Spread a blanket on the grass, lie down, and draw her down beside him. Lean over her and watch the play of light on her face through leaves that were turning crimson and gold. Thread his hands through her hair. Feed her half of his sandwich. Have her feed him half of hers. Watch her sit up to drink the wine. Press her down and lean over her to kiss her and taste the lingering sweetness of the wine on her lips.

"Are you still speaking to me?" In the evening, a little after six, the doorbell of Rana's apartment had rung insistently. She opened the door to find Kris, a chastened Kris, still in her business clothes, a lightweight cream suit and a blazing red blouse, her face drawn in an apprehensive look that went straight to Rana's heart.

"I was on my way home from work and I thought . . . I thought I should come and talk to you."

"Come in." Rana stepped back and watched as Kris moved past her into the living room.

"I wanted you to know that I—" Kris's head swung around, her perusal slow, her face registering her shock. "What have you been doing?"

"Buying things. Sit down."

"Why have you been buying things?" Kris said, gingerly lowering herself to the couch and rubbing her hand over the velvet material.

"Would you believe I don't know?"

"I could never understand why you didn't have any furniture in the first place."

Rana pushed back a lock of shiny brown hair. "I didn't understand it myself. I'm glad you came, Kris."

Kris peered at her anxiously. "You don't look very good. Are you all right?"

Rana murmured, "Second opinion confirms diagnosis."

"What?"

Rana gave her a rueful look. "That very same sentiment was expressed earlier today by my friend downstairs. And it didn't come on a get-well card."

"I'm not sure I know what you're talking about."

"Skip it. It isn't important."

Kris honed the knife. "Does the way you look have anything to do with Luc Garrett?"

She thought about lying. It wasn't that she didn't want to. She just didn't have the strength. "It has everything to do with Luc Garrett. Can I get you some iced tea?"

"Only if I get to follow you out into the kitchen and keep grilling you."

"Wouldn't you rather help me grill a couple of steaks instead? Can you stay for dinner?"

"I shouldn't, but . . . if you insist. Steve is working late tonight, and I hate to spend the evening alone."

141

Out in the kitchen Kris took off her jacket. Rana gave her a coverall apron made out of beige poplin, and while Kris tied it on, Rana took the salad ingredients out of the refrigerator. Kris stood at the sink and washed the lettuce and then perched in a high chair next to the snack bar with a board and the rest of the salad ingredients in front of her. Rana handed her a knife, and Kris began to chop at a furious tempo as she said, "Now tell me about the luscious Luc."

Rana took the steaks out and unwrapped them, thankful that her back was to Kris. "There's nothing to tell."

"Rana—" The tone was unbelieving.

"Really, Kris."

Kris took a breath. "Remember how off-the-wall I was after David asked for a divorce? And remember how you listened to me until I got it all out of my system? I poured everything out to you. And after that, you refused to let me sit around and mope. Get out, you said. You're not dead. Get back into the land of the living."

"If there's anything I hate, it's being quoted out of context."

Kris stared at Rana's shiny brown cap of hair. "You're not going to escape that easily, my friend. A few quips will not get you out of this. So. After I had bared my soul to you for days on end, you finally got tired of the whole thing and told me we were going out to a concert. That night I met Steve."

"So you see? I was right."

"Yes, about me. But I wasn't. That's my point. We can't see our own lives clearly because we're right in the middle of them."

"Luc Garrett has nothing to do with my life."

Kris stopped chopping and looked up at Rana. "I saw that television program, you know."

"That was a . . . an accident. . . ."

"I know how it happened. Steve knew somebody who was at the party and saw the whole thing."

"Sometimes this *big* town seems like a very *small* town," Rana murmured wryly.

"And when they showed those photographs"—the knife stopped chunking against the board—"I looked at Luc's face. Rana, that man was enjoying every minute of your little altercation on the floor."

"He wasn't enjoying it a few seconds later."

"Maybe not. But then the way he defended you after that— Rana, have some sense. A man doesn't take abuse like that for a woman he doesn't care for. Have you got a bowl for this?"

Her hands shaking, Rana dug a brown pottery bowl out of the cupboard, wondering if Kris was ever going to stop this interrogation. How much more could she take? Yet Rana couldn't, wouldn't, run the risk of offending her, since Kris had come to mend the breach between them. Rana had to stay cool —and say as little as possible.

The delicate aroma of the spice that Rana had sprinkled on the steaks filled the kitchen. Kris closed her eyes. "Umm, does that smell good. I'm glad I picked tonight to ease my conscience."

"So am I. I've missed you, Kris."

"And I've felt like a grade A heel, mostly because I just— well, Luc Garrett is a gorgeous man. But anybody can see how he feels about you."

"Can they?" she said dryly.

"Of course. The man adores you. There," she said, lifting the bowl and putting it in the refrigerator so it would stay cold until the steaks cooked. "Salad's all done. Now what? Can I set the table?"

"Yes, if you like."

When the steaks were done, and they sat down at the round table to eat, Kris said, "So why aren't you two together?"

Rana glanced up from her plate. "Don't you ever give up?"

"Not on something as important as your love life."

"I don't have a love life."

"I would take a wager against high odds that Luc Garrett would like to change that."

"I . . . couldn't let him do that."

"Why not?" Kris picked up on Rana's tension immediately. "Has he asked you already? And you turned him down? Oh, Rana, how could you?"

Rana laid her fork down on her plate, her appetite gone. She had to close off this discussion somehow. And the best way was with the truth. "I can't . . . take the chance of . . . hurting him."

Kris stared at her, her mouth agape. "What are you talking about?"

Rana shook her head, her throat too full to talk.

"Rana O'Neill." Kris sat back. "You mean to sit there and tell me you're keeping Luc Garrett out of your life because of what happened to your parents?"

Rana met her stare, her face stricken. "If you care for someone"—her voice low—"the last thing in the world you want to do is destroy them. If I can prevent that from happening to Luc, I will. In any way I can."

Kris tossed her napkin on the table and, gazing at Rana, shook her head. "I don't believe it. You've got to be the best candidate for the nuthouse I've ever seen walking around loose."

"I know it isn't logical . . . or even sensible. I just know that if I . . . if I let him into my life, we could end up destroying each other." Rana got up from the table and walked to the coffee server. She needed something to do, some way to expend her nervous tension. She picked up the glass carafe and walked back to the table to fill Kris's cup. "Don't you see?" she said, turning to replace the server and then clutching the cupboard, facing away from Kris, saying the words to the wall. "All the same elements are there. Our facility with words. Our careers. The public curiosity we generate." In a low voice that Kris had to strain to hear, Rana said, "He's even writing a play."

There was a long silence. Then Kris said, "Rana, listen to me. Please. Turn around and listen to me."

When Rana complied, Kris captured Rana's eyes with a

straight look and said, "You know I tease you a lot—but I have great respect for your intelligence."

Rana made a dismissive gesture with her hand.

"No, I mean it. You're a smart lady, and I envy you every time I read your column. But you're missing something really important here." Kris's shoulders moved under the red silk. "Knowing you're intelligent, knowing you can make up your own mind about things, I'm just going to say what's on my mind and you can—take it or leave it, whichever you like. But I've got to say it. Because I have a debt to you, one that I can never repay . . . unless you think there's something in what I'm going to say."

"Go on."

"You're forgetting one vital fact. You have a big advantage your parents didn't have." Kris took a breath. "You *saw* what happened to them." Kris was quiet for a moment, watching Rana absorb the thought. "You saw how they used their talent with words to mess up their lives. Do you honestly think you and Luc would go the same route when you already know what's at the end of that road?"

Rana looked stunned. After a moment she said huskily, "I'd do anything to prevent it."

"Exactly. Rana, you learned from your parents' experience. And you learned your lesson very well. Look at you. You're all hollow-eyed and unhappy and putting yourself through hell because you're afraid that you might—*might* hurt Luc. Isn't that a strong indication that your love for him is pretty tough stuff?"

Rana shook her head. "I . . . How can I be sure of that?"

Kris made a sound of disgust. "What do you want—a signed decree from a bona fide source in heaven that says you and Luc will never hurt each other?" Kris shook her head. "When two people try to blend their lives together, there are bound to be some rough edges. Sometimes they get tired and irritable and bored and say things they don't mean. But that doesn't mean they love each other any less.

"You have to take a chance, Rana. Just like everybody else.

145

You have to step off that high board and free-fall into a relationship just like every other woman does, the way I did with Steve. Men don't come with guarantees."

Kris's words brought the dream Rana had dreamed to her mind, the vivid dream where she had been poised on a diving board over Luc Garrett's arms. She said, "Women don't come with guarantees, either."

"No," Kris agreed, her mouth turning up at the corner, "that's true. Luc isn't getting any prize with you." Kris smiled to take the sting out of the dry, teasing words. "But on the other hand, he's an ideal candidate to put up with your idiosyncrasies. He'll probably even think that glazed look you get in your eye is kind of cute. When you're irritable, he'll know it's because the writing isn't going well. And you will know enough to let him alone when he's on a long roll and churning out pages of the final pulse-pounding moments of his book. Give him a chance, Rana." Kris paused. "And give yourself a chance. Trust yourself."

"I don't think I . . . can."

Kris stared at her for a moment and then got briskly to her feet. She took off the apron and laid it over the back of her chair, her eyes avoiding Rana's. "Well, I suppose it doesn't make any difference, really," she said, in a tone that sounded odd to Rana's ears. "But it's obvious you need some male companionship or something to get you out of this apartment. Why don't you give Phil a call?"

The thought of talking to Phil, going out with him, having him touch her casually as he helped her out of the car or guided her down the aisle of a theater made her physically ill.

Kris looked at her with a gleam of satisfaction simmering in her eyes. "Well, it was just a suggestion."

After that final thrust Kris sailed out of the kitchen and went into the living room. Still reeling from Kris's double-edged onslaught, Rana followed. Kris said, "I'd help you with the dishes, but if I stay, I'll start feeling sorry for you." She turned and looked at Rana. "You don't deserve that. Not when one telephone call would bring Luc Garrett to your door this evening. You are a lady who doesn't deserve one ounce of sympathy."

"You seem very sure of his . . . involvement."

"Hey." Kris gestured with her thumb up. "I know a besotted guy when I see one. He wanted to eat you alive that day in the Hyatt, but instead he had to go and have lunch with his editor. And you ran like a scared rabbit out in the street for a taxi. There were very strong vibes there—and this was long before you two ended up on the floor together in front of half the television viewing audience of America." At Rana's expression Kris held her hand up. "I know, I know. I'm shutting up. And I'm going. I wouldn't want you to use your lethal karate expertise to throw me out into the hall."

A few minutes later, after Kris had gone, Rana turned back to the suddenly quiet apartment. Easy. Yes, easy for Kris to say . . . go to him. Easy to pick up the phone. Easy to . . . think that this time . . . this time it would be all right . . . so easy to say, I want him. I need him. Therefore, it is right. . . .

Her nerves singing with tension, she walked a very wide path around the telephone and went back out into the kitchen and began to clear the table.

CHAPTER EIGHT

When Rana came home the next day after doing research at the library, Luc was there outside her apartment building, the grocery bag still in his hand, the loaf of bread in its white wrapper poking out at the exact same angle. The weather was unseasonably warm, and in his short-sleeved knit shirt and khaki pants he looked wonderful, as soul-destroying as ever. Her legs ached with the effort it took to keep from running to him. Worse, one glance told her his face echoed the agony she felt.

Knowing she wouldn't be able to resist him if he came nearer, she crossed the street to avoid passing by him. He frowned darkly and started toward her, but before he could reach her, she hurried into the foyer of her building.

Her heart pounding, her legs weak, she reached forward and punched the elevator button. She half-expected his hand to come from behind and catch her elbow. It didn't.

She ate her solitary evening meal and cleaned up the kitchen, and as she did so, the silverware clacked loudly against the cupboard and the dishes rattled against the sink, making her jump. Her nerves were on edge. She was wound up tight, and there was no way to ease her tension.

When she finished the dishes, she knew she could no longer avoid the inevitable. She had to see Luc and ask him to please, please, stop following her. Just that. No more.

She went into the bedroom and opened her closet door, telling herself she was looking for something cool to wear. In the back, behind her sensible suits and dresses, was a cotton gauze outfit she had sent for on an impulse and never worn, a lounging suit from Cyprus. The creamy two-piece set transformed her into a modern resident of the sultan's palace. The top was elasticized in a round neckline that could be worn on the shoulder or off. She kept it on her shoulders and added a wide copper slave bracelet below one elbow-length sleeve. The pants were voluminous except over her hips and abdomen where a smooth-fitting triangle of lace had been inserted into the fabric. The harem look was completed by the balloon-shaped legs caught at the ankle and the two tiny tassels that were attached to the bottom of the blouse and dangled over her flat stomach. With flat sandals and a tasseled bag that matched the mood of her costume, she hurried out of her apartment . . . before she lost her nerve.

The theater was dark, the only light pouring over the seats coming from the stage, just as it had been the night Luc had taken her there. Rehearsal was in progress, and there were two actors on stage, a man and a woman. She felt like an interloper and yet . . . she couldn't leave.

No one seemed to notice her, and no one questioned her presence. She stood and looked around the tiny theater—and found the dark head she was seeking. Luc sat slumped sideways in a seat that was dead center in the empty rows.

She took a breath and began to walk down the aisle, her whole being focused on Luc, her nerves pulsing with awareness. The two little tassels bounced against her body. Her heart thudded so hard in her chest that she felt as if her body shook with each beat.

Suppose he didn't want to see her? Suppose, after she had run away from him this afternoon, he had begun to hate her? Suppose . . . On the other side of him in the seat sat the brown bag with its ludicrous bundle of bread.

She turned and began to thread through the seats toward Luc. When she reached the one next to him, she sank down into it and fastened her gaze on the stage. He didn't move or look up at her.

In an agony of suspense, she said, "Hello, Luc."

He didn't flicker an eyelash. He sat as still as marble, his eyes fastened on the stage. "What are you doing here?"

She turned to look at him. That dark face, that well-molded jaw, that wonderful mouth might have been carved of stone. He sat just as he was, slumped back in a corner of the seat, his eyes fastened on the stage as if he couldn't tear them away. With that terrible intuitiveness she had about him, she realized he was afraid to look at her . . . because he didn't know what she was going to say.

"I have this problem," she said softly.

"Is it serious?"

Luc knew if he moved he'd lash out at her in his anger and hurt. He didn't know why she was here, but he knew she hadn't come to tell him she'd changed her mind. And just to sit next to her and not reach out and grab was pure hell.

She wanted to weep. He was so guarded, so wary. He was protecting himself. And why shouldn't he? She'd already hurt him once. How could she do it again? She said, "Well, you see, this man is following me."

"Have the police arrest him," he said in a cool tone that made her stomach twist in pain.

"Well, it isn't that simple," she said lightly. "You see, he has this bag full of groceries with this loaf of Italian bread sticking out the top."

"Are you sure?"

"Quite sure."

"It might be French bread"—in a flat tone that made it impossible to tell if he was joking.

"No," she said, smiling a faint smile, her eyes flickering to the bag beside him. "I'm positive it's Italian."

"I don't believe it," he said carefully.

"You see? Neither will the police"—more anxiously—"do you think?"

He considered it. "Probably not."

151

Silence. Then she said, "I thought perhaps . . . you might help me."

He didn't move a muscle. "Why should I?"

"Because," she swallowed, "this man is haunting me."

"Umm. Sounds like you're being shadowed by the Spaghetti Spector."

She clasped her fingers together in her lap, afraid to laugh . . . afraid to hope. "Are you sure?"

"I'd have to investigate more thoroughly." Slowly, deliberately, he turned his head, his eyes claiming hers, their gleam unmistakably predatory. "We may have to spend some time together—working on it."

She was lost. As she knew she was. As she knew she had always been, right from the beginning.

"What would you suggest"—she reached out to touch him tentatively, her fingers aching to feel the warm strength of his that lay on the arm of the chair between them—"as the first step?"

"The first step," he said, his hand closing over hers, "is to get the hell out of here."

His fingers clasping hers in a grip that felt as if he wouldn't let go of her again soon, he stood up and dragged her up with him. "Hey, Ted. Catch this thing, will you?"

He reached in and picked up the bread with his left hand and tossed it like a football toward the stage. The woman on the stage turned to stare out in the darkness at him as the bread fell to the floor with a thud.

Rana swiveled around, her eyes laughing up at him. "It sounded like it was made out of stone."

"Stage prop."

"You've been walking around the streets of New York looking like the original street waif, making me feel sorry for you, with a *stage prop?*" She began to pommel him with her free hand. All the action on the stage stopped as the couple turned to stare at them.

"By the time I broke down your resistance, the real thing

would have been a bag of bread crumbs." He caught the hand that was punishing him and began to push her sideways along in front of the seats toward the aisle. "No physical confrontation in the theater. That's a rule. It's printed on a posted list backstage."

"You big fake," she got out through choking laughter. "You double-died phony. You let me think . . ." Dissolving, melting, she struggled to free herself unsuccessfully as he dragged her with him up the aisle toward the lobby. Behind them, someone yelled, "Attaboy, Luc. Show her who's boss. But watch out for that shoulder pinch."

The laughter and the voices faded behind them. Outside in the lobby, alone in front of the picture of Bette Davis, Luc turned her into his arms. "The bread was fake. The feeling was not." He loosened her hands and cupped her face in his, devouring her with his eyes. "Kiss me, Rana. Hold me. My God, I've been waiting so damn long. . . ."

She slid her arms around his waist and fit her body into the wonderful, well-remembered niche in Luc's arms that seemed made for her. "No longer than I have been," she murmured against his mouth.

She pressed closer, trying to absorb the wonderful essence of him, the feel, the taste, the smell of him, into every cell of her being.

"What the hell?" He pulled away from her. "What are these?" His fingers tugged at the tassels that had butted up against his lean stomach.

"I'm surprised you didn't recognize them." Her gray eyes shone. "They're the sesame seeds for the bread," she said, and pulled his head down to her mouth.

Inside his apartment he turned her into his arms. Against his mouth, she murmured, "Luc, I have a confession to make."

"I'm not interested," he said, kissing her lips, gently, so very gently.

"Please." She drew away from him slightly. "You must. I . . . have a spectre of my own."

153

The trembling note in her voice made him stop kissing her. He drew back slightly to look down into her face with a tender seriousness that melted that last bit of defense she thought she had erected against him. He said, "Actually, you have two of them, don't you?"

She nodded and then dropped her head against his chest. "Please try to understand if I . . . only have enough courage to share this one night with you."

His hands tightened painfully on her arms, but his voice was bland. "Warning me off already, sweetheart?"

"I . . . have to be honest with you. I just don't know . . . I can't . . . I don't want to hurt you."

There was an electric silence. Then he said in a dark voice that trembled with intensity, "Of all the women I have ever known, you are the only one who has ever worried about me and what I might be feeling. . . ." He bent suddenly and lifted her off her feet. Her brown hair fell in a silken mass over his arm.

He began to walk. She closed her eyes and lay cradled against his chest, the echo of his words like a weight on her, the steady beat of his heart pounding against her ear. She knew where his long strides were taking them.

When he turned a corner, she opened her eyes. Behind them the door was conveniently open—and in front of her, the bed was unmade, the brown sheets open and inviting.

"I'm not the neatest of people," he said smoothly, walking with her toward the bed. "And I must admit that after this afternoon, not even in my wildest dreams did I think I would be walking into this bedroom tonight with you in my arms."

"Luc, listen to me. You've got to understand that the odds are against us. . . ."

"The odds are against us doing what? Sharing each other? Laughing together? Crying together? Wrestling? Making love?" He smiled that wonderful Luc smile and laid her down on the bed, nestling her into the pillow that he had lain in the night before, watching with a deep satisfaction as she turned her

154

mouth into his palm. "We've already done everything except the last . . . and the odds on that are dropping drastically minute by minute."

She turned her head to look at him, those gray eyes dark and disturbed. "Surviving, Luc. I'm talking about surviving."

He laughed suddenly, his teeth flashing white in his tanned face. "Oh, honey," he said, nudging her over to fit a lean hip against her side as he sat next to her, bending closer and tugging at the tassel that lay in a very interesting place, "I think the odds are good that we'll survive." He toyed with the tassel, his eyes brilliant. "Does this thing serve a useful purpose or is it purely—for decoration?" He grinned roguishly and stretched the tassel out full length down across her abdomen and let his fingers rest where it came to a stop. "Or should I say it's impurely for decoration?"

His hand on her sent a stinging warmth through her. She put a hand up to touch him, tracing along a laugh line beside his mouth. His amusement seemed layered over a face that had grown older, a little more lined in the last few weeks, and she knew she had been the cause of his unhappiness. "Luc," she whispered, "don't talk any more. Please, just kiss—"

With a soft, guttural sound, he bent his head and brought his mouth down to hers. He explored her lips, caressing, nipping her lower one lightly with his teeth, teasing her with his tongue and bringing a sensual moan to her throat and making her push at him with her hands to relieve the agonizing ecstasy.

He shook his head in answer to her unsuccessful attempt to pull away from him. "No, Rana. Tonight you're going to forget your memories. Tonight you're going to forget who you are and who I am—"

"No, Luc, don't ask me to do that. I can't forget—"

"Rana—"

"No, hear me out, Luc. I can't forget who I am because . . . I don't want to. You make me feel more of what I am, more alive, more real, more . . . me."

His eyes flared into brilliant blue flames. "Then fly with me,

155

honey." He laid a hand lightly on her bare shoulder and brushed the edge of her blouse down. Her eyes darkened as his hand moved on her pale, cool skin. She trembled and looked at him out of dark eloquent eyes, but said nothing. "No, don't hold back. Tell me what you're thinking. Don't ever hold back with me, Rana. Not now. Not ever."

"Do you know what I told myself before I went out tonight?" He shook his head and waited.

"I told myself that I was going to tell you to stop following me. But when I saw you, I . . . I couldn't do it."

He groaned and leaned forward to press his mouth to hers for a brief, hard kiss. "Thank God you had the courage to recognize the truth." He pulled at the other shoulder of her blouse, gently baring a tiny bit more of the delicate, creamy flesh. Her tempo of breathing changed. He saw it, and, chuckling in pure enjoyment, ran his finger just above the material, finding the sloping tops of her smooth, curved flesh.

"You're like a sunrise," he breathed, "one that's just beginning, full of light and color and fresh air."

He tugged again at the pliant cotton and slanted it downward, baring the sweet curve of one breast completely. Her eyes darkened, and she raised her hand instinctively. He caught it and brought it up to his mouth. "You know," he said, in a husky, reflective voice, his lips moving against her palm, "I keep having this dream. Instead of my undressing you, I dream that you're undressing me. Then you put me in the shower, and I drag you in with me while you still have your clothes on."

"Sounds bizarre," she said in as serious a tone as she could manage while the laughter bubbled inside and his fingers played over her breast in ever smaller circles. "Have you considered consulting a psychiatrist?"

"He'd only tell me I was going crazy, and I already knew that. I was losing my mind, wanting you, wanting you so much. . . ." Gently, from underneath, he caressed the hard bud that tightened in readiness for him with fingers that knew exactly how to tantalize and tease. Mysteriously, her other breast was freed to his roving hands, and she was caught in a storm of delight.

"Have I told you I like your choice of attire?" he said huskily. "Lift your arms, honey. Let me—ah yes, that's it." He divested her of the top and rewarded her cooperation by kissing her lightly on the mouth and running his tongue over hers.

He drew away and looked down at her flushed beauty. "Comfortable, honey?"

She glanced at him, puzzled. "Your bed is very comfortable. Why?"

"I thought"—here the smile again—"you might be too warm."

"Did you?" Her fingers traced the line of buttons down his shirt. "And what would happen if I was?"

"I'd help you off with a few more items of your clothing."

"The ever-thoughtful Luc Garrett."

"My mother always said I was the considerate one. You might even agree, since you were treated to a sampling of my brother's rudeness." He inserted his fingers in her trousers and began to draw them down over her. He dealt quickly with the extra elastic fastening at the ankles and tossed the cotton trousers on the floor.

"Yes," he breathed softly, his eyes moving over her slender body clad only in the cream silk bikinis. "You definitely look more comfortable."

"But you don't. You look too warm." She began to unbutton his shirt, her fingers brushing lightly over the fine hairs of his chest as she pulled each button free. She reached the last button, and slowly she pulled his shirt away from his pants, touching him with delicate, light fingers as she worked.

His breathing altered. She unbuttoned his cuffs and sat up to pull the shirt off of him.

His eyes played over the gracefulness of her body in motion. "Strange," he said, "how having you take my shirt off me makes me feel warmer than ever."

157

"Then I'd better try your pants. Maybe I'll have better luck with them," she said huskily.

"I doubt it," he said, in that deep, velvet voice. "But far be it from me to interfere with a scientific experiment."

"How very noble of you." He wore the same buckle that he had worn the night she had undressed him and put him in the shower, and because she was familiar with the little clip on the back, even though he was sitting down, she unhooked it easily.

"You seem quite . . . adept at this."

Without thinking, she said, "I've done it before."

His tender smile disappeared. He grasped her shoulders and pushed her back on the bed. "That's a hell of a thing to say."

She stared up at him, her eyes dark and anguished.

"Say what you're thinking," he said through gritted teeth.

Knowing that this was the first hurdle, she said lightly, "Even when you don't want to hear it?"

He closed his eyes as if her words had struck him in a vital place. Then he let go of her shoulders, but he stared down at her in a gaze that kept her pinned to the bed. "Yes, even when I don't want to hear it." He made an anguished sound and turned his head away, his dark brown hair gleaming in the light. "Oh, God. I don't have any right to judge you."

"No, you don't," she said in a soft, gentle tone, reaching up to catch his head with both her hands and bring his face back around to her, her thumbs finding and stroking the hard cheekbones. "I know how to unfasten your buckle because—"

He groaned and moved toward her to kiss her. "No, don't. You don't have to explain a damn thing to me. It's none of my business."

"But I want to." She pushed him away from her a little in order to look directly into his eyes. "I want you to understand that what you're thinking isn't true."

"It isn't necessary—"

Exasperated, she said, "Will you listen to me? It is necessary." She sighed. "I unfastened it once before—on you—the night I came here to your apartment. What you remembered

158

wasn't a dream, Luc. I really did undress you and put you in the shower. At least," she smiled faintly, a tentative smile that tore his heart out of his chest, "I tried to."

He gathered her into his arms, crushing her softness against his hard chest. "Oh, God. I've got so much to learn about you."

She buried her head in the hollow of his neck and said in a muffled voice, "You really mean that, don't you?"

"Oh, yes," he murmured, pulling away from her to look at her. "I mean it. I want to learn everything about you." He laid her down gently on the pillow and stroked her hair. "Starting now." His hand trailed down over her throat, wandered over her shoulder, his eyes never leaving her face. "And not just physically, Rana. I want to know what pleases you, what displeases you. I want to know if you drink orange juice in the morning and wake up with a smile on your face—or if you're unapproachable until you've had your coffee." Lower, lower over the silken skin, until he reached one creamy breast. He leaned down and kissed the hollow of her throat, his thumb finding and caressing the dark prize at the center of her breast. He lifted away from her a little and watched with satisfaction as her hips moved in response to the tremors that coursed through her. He leaned over her again, and the light brush of his hair sent pleasure waves rippling over her . . . and then his mouth claimed her. The moist warmth of his lips and tongue played over that sensitive crest and sent heated tongues of desire radiating upward from her abdomen where his hand lay lightly on the silken barrier she still wore.

"I can remember one morning you woke up in a very bad mood."

She wasn't ready just yet to tell him why. She didn't want to think about Luc's other lovers. That was another hurdle yet to cross. "If you really want to know me," she said in a faint husk of voice, "you'll have to learn that I never leave a job unfinished."

"What?" He pulled away in surprise.

"You interrupted me while I was conducting an experiment."

159

His dawning smile of comprehension was roguish. With a great show of reluctance, he straightened and braced his hands on the bed on either side of her, making his waist accessible to her. "Conduct away, lady."

The buckle was the same, but the pants weren't. They were khaki, with a fastener she didn't understand, and by the time she finally did, he was chuckling softly. "Not all that experienced, are you?" he drawled.

"I think we've already covered that subject."

"But I didn't really find out anything about your past loves," he said lightly.

"You know the only important thing about them that you need to know," she said in an equally light tone. "They are in the past. I might"—his zipper came down—"ask you the same thing."

"I have only one, and as yet I haven't quite"—he stopped, obviously searching for the correct words—"tasted all her delights."

"But you seem quite accustomed to waking up in the morning with female company beside you." There, she had said it. "You were only surprised when you saw it was me."

His eyes bright with comprehension, he stood up and kicked off his loafers and stepped out of his pants. His bikinis were a matching khaki color. He sat back down beside her, lifted her chin with his warm fingers, and looked down into those glimmering, silvery eyes. "So that's why you were so angry with me that morning. I thought it was because I'd been drinking and passed out on you."

"No, you're quite adorable when you're under the influence of alcohol, Luc."

He leaned over her and smiled. "It's only when I'm sober you can't stand me?"

"Would I be here with you like this if I couldn't stand you?"

He smiled that roguish smile at her, and drawled, "Woman, your logic is breathtaking." He leaned closer. "Along with your other—scenic delights." He pressed a kiss on the peak of her breast and then raised his head to look at her, still half lying on her. Bare and hard, his weight pressing her into the softness of the bed, he sent her body into stinging life. Heated need coursed through her veins everywhere he touched her.

She clasped his naked shoulders, wanting him very badly. "Do you know something, Luc Garrett? You talk too much."

"And you," he said softly, "have not completed your work."

"Work?" She couldn't think what he was talking about. His mouth was making havoc of her thinking, moving over her, brushing lightly on first one breast and then the other, then down to her navel, moving along the outline of her bikinis, and back up on a path through the hollow concave of her abdomen. He said, "You haven't finished undressing me."

Those khaki bikinis. "Luc, I—"

"You never," he said softly, "leave a job undone. That's what you told me. Are you a woman of your word—or not?"

He'd delivered the challenge flawlessly, he knew that. He waited, breath held. She was a dazzling creature with her brown hair loose over her shoulders and her eyes shimmering with sensual radiance.

She flashed him a defiant glance that sent a shock of pleasure coursing through him. She was such a beautiful combination of sweetness and spirit. How had she escaped being claimed? Had she held everyone at bay but him?

He's the only one, she thought. He's the only one who's ever had the courage to talk to me, look at me, love me like this. . . .

She said, "Stand up, Luc."

He obeyed immediately. With hands that trembled, she took hold of the edges of his underpants and drew them down, her cool fingers tracing the length of his hard thighs and calves.

He sank down on the bed to sit beside her. "And now you."

How gentle his hands were! And how right it felt to have Luc taking away the last bit of cloth from her body.

"Rana." He lay down beside her and contentedly adored her

161

with his eyes, touring her visually, seeking out the beauty that was his.

The need to touch became too strong. She reached for him and he, her. His hands explored, discovering the crevice behind her ears, the sensitivity of the nape of her neck, the rosy peaks that waited for him. His mouth completed the journey of discovery, moving in a slow, sensuous circle, his tongue caressing one breast and then the other, the warm moistness building, building the intolerable ache. When she thought she could stand no more, his hand trailed across her stomach to that silkiness between her thighs where his fingers sought and found the treasure.

She made a sound, a soft animal noise of anticipation. He probed deeper, more expertly, bringing a sharp sigh of ecstasy to her lips.

"Luc, I didn't expect to feel this way."

"What way?" He watched her, fascinated with the expressions that crossed her face, the agonized delight, the attempt to hold onto sanity, the sliding back into the intense concentration on her body's response to his touch.

Rana sank her fingers into the hard muscles of his shoulders, caught between pleading for him to stop . . . and begging him to go on spinning that web of mindless delight.

The lovely magic went on, inexorably bringing her closer to the edge of wanton madness. She moved restlessly, trying to ease the intolerable ache. "So . . . hungry. So empty. Please, Luc . . ."

He shook his head, chuckling under his breath. "Such impatience. The balance of power is mine right now, honey. You've given it to me. Trust me, Rana. Let me show you how it can be between a man and a woman who aren't afraid to enjoy each other."

He fanned the flame, making the fire rise higher. In desperation, she reached out and flattened her hands on his chest, rubbing the male nipples back and forth with her palms. They rose and hardened under her touch. Triumphant, she let her hands wander over him, feeling the hard muscles of his stomach and the hair-crisp skin of his thighs.

"I think the balance of power has just shifted," he murmured in a husky rasp.

"To me?" She went on caressing him, letting her hands wander.

"To you."

She was lovely and pliant, and her hands worked a heady magic and brought him to a height that even he, in his years of experience, had never quite reached before. He needed her desperately. No longer able to prolong the agony, he moved over her and made her his.

He lay with the back of his hand on her abdomen, his wrist on her hip bone.

"Luc?"

"Umm."

"Are you going to call a cab?"

"What shall I call it?"

"Expensive," she murmured under her breath, remembering and smiling.

He turned his head and looked at her. "What did you say?"

"It wasn't important." He accepted that and closed his eyes. She lay there gazing at him, feasting her eyes on his lazily sated male beauty. More silence. "Luc?"

"Yes?" The drawl, long, drawn out, his eyes still closed.

"I'd better go."

"Why? Don't you like the accommodations here?"

"The accommodations are fine. It's just that I . . . I think it would be better if I went now."

All the lazy lethargy disappeared. He came up out of the bed and lunged, leaning over her to prop himself on the hard hand next to her ribs, trapping her. "You're not going anywhere."

She put her hand up to touch his face. He gazed down at her in amazement. How was it that this woman could melt him with just the brush of her fingertips? She said in a soft, husky tone, "I warned you how it would be."

Everything about her called up his protective instincts: the bare, brazen beauty of her body, the tousled length of brown hair his hands had caressed, the faintly dazzled look his love-making had given her that still lingered in her eyes. "You can't walk away from me. Not now." The need to kiss her, caress her, became overpowering. He lowered his mouth and gently touched her lips with the tip of his tongue. She tasted hot and satiny. "Not now."

"Later?" Her resistance was gone. She said the word only to save her pride.

His tongue probed insistently, found entrance, teased and enticed. He wanted her again, he thought incredibly. She had given him an insatiable thirst—that only she could ease. "Much later," he murmured. She didn't argue.

When she woke again around noon, she found him lying beside her, watching her lazily, one finger tracing a path down her arm. "Luc, I've got to go home. I've got a column to write."

"Don't you always," he said, his finger reversing directions, going up her arm to crest at her shoulder and slide down to the top of her breast.

Tiny shivers rose under his finger. "Luc, I've got to get up."

He watched in apparent fascination as her body responded to his tickling touch. "Why?"

"I just told you. I've got a column to write."

He traced a widening circle on her abdomen, watching with interest as the shivers rose in his wake. "Do it here. I'll bring my typewriter in and set it up here for you."

She shook her head. "I can't let you do that. I have to go back to my own apartment. I'm expecting a repairman to look at my computer, and if I'm not there . . . Luc, I can't think when you touch me like that."

"Good. Too much thinking is bad for the brain." He touched her other breast with that same, marauding fingertip.

"But the repairman said he was coming today."

He looked complacent, not the least bit worried about her repairman. He seemed far more interested in the path of the goose bumps traveling across her body that betrayed her responsiveness to his touch. "The calendar and the clock. The tyrannical gods of civilization."

"Are you always so philosophical in bed?"

"There's only one way to find out for sure." He closed the discussion by kissing her.

Much later he murmured in her ear, "Are you hungry?" His breath moved her hair.

She stretched lazily. "I suppose I should be. What time is it?"

"If I tell you, will you promise not to panic?"

Her eyes opened wider. "What time is it, Luc?"

"Four o'clock?"

"Four o'clock!" She sat up, the sheet falling to her waist. "In the afternoon?"

"You're panicking, honey. Beautifully, I must admit, but nevertheless, panicking." His eyes roved over her bare curves.

"Luc, I've got to go."

"I'll come home with you."

She tried to talk him out of it after she had showered and dressed, but he insisted on going with her to her apartment. Once there, he had her show him around her kitchen, and then he told her to leave him. He owed her a spaghetti dinner, he told her, and he was a man who paid his debts.

He was also a terrible cook. He burned the spaghetti and put too much oregano in the sauce. They ended up eating grilled cheese sandwiches and falling asleep in each other's arms in her bed.

In the morning Luc called the repairman. Luc spoke softly into the telephone, but there was a frost in his voice that made her glad she wasn't on the receiving end of his incisive comments.

When he hung up the phone, he said coolly, "Your man will

165

be out this afternoon. I'm going home to pack up a few things. I'll be back—"

"Luc—" She caught his arm. "We haven't discussed living together."

He looked at her, his blue eyes cool and practical. "No," he said, "we haven't. Is there any reason we should discuss it?"

His logic seemed impeccable. "You mean you're just going to move in—right now? Without discussing it with me?"

"You came to me, Rana, just as I said you would. For the duration, at least, you've let me into your life. Do you plan to throw me out of it now?"

"No," she said on a soft whisper of sound that he almost didn't hear.

"I plan to spend my nights with you. Would you like me to run back and forth between two apartments?" he asked blandly.

"No, that wouldn't be fair."

"Are you afraid of what people might say?"

"No, I don't care about that but—"

"You don't want a long term commitment," he said, watching her carefully. "Is that it?"

"Yes, I . . . Luc, you know that's impossible."

Dark lashes drifted over his eyes. "I'll only be in New York until a few days after the play opens. Suppose we try . . . staying together . . . until then? Is that open-ended enough for you?"

"I . . ." She thought about sending him away—and knew she couldn't do it. "I suppose that would be all right."

"Then it's settled." He kissed her, lifting her against him, tasting her with his mouth and tongue until he had her clinging to him and sighing with need. "Is there anything else you wanted to discuss?"

If there was, she had forgotten it. Luc's kiss had blown everything out of her head. He smiled and said, "Good. I'll be back this afternoon with my things."

CHAPTER NINE

The repairman came, fixed Rana's computer, presented her with a healthy bill, and left. Rana didn't know whether it was by accident or design, but Luc did not return until two hours later. He arrived at her door carrying a small suitcase in one hand and his typewriter in the other.

He set his suitcase down and walked toward her. She stood as if frozen and then suddenly came to life. She dodged his reaching arms adroitly, picked up his case, and headed toward the bedroom. From inside she said to him over her shoulder, "I've cleared out a drawer for you in the bureau." She put his case on the floor and moved away from him to look into the bathroom as if she needed to assure herself that there was nothing of hers lying around. "There are towels in this cabinet underneath the sink, and the clothes hamper is here—did you plan on sharing laundry duty?" She turned around in the door of the bathroom and smiled brightly at him. When he moved toward her, she slipped past him again and walked out of the bedroom into the hallway. "I have my computer in the spare room which I use as my office. We can set your typewriter up in there on another table. And of course you'll need a spare key. I think I have one that I tossed into a drawer out in the kitchen—"

He put an arm across the doorway and trapped her inside. "Stop sounding like the tour guide on a cruise ship."

She bristled, her eyes flashing angrily up at him. He felt vastly relieved. Any emotional reaction was better than her bright, paper-thin formality. She said, "I'm sorry if I don't have all the right words."

167

Moving like lightning, he dropped his arm and pulled her into his embrace. "You don't have to have the 'right' words. All I need from you is the truth." He wrapped her closer in his arms. "Say what you're really feeling, Rana."

There in his arms, his blue eyes blazing down into hers, she couldn't do anything else. "I'm afraid, Luc."

"Beautiful," he murmured. "Say it again."

"I'm afraid." Her arms around his waist tightened.

"Louder," he murmured. She obeyed. "You're doing beautifully, honey." He lowered his head, and his mouth moved over hers lightly, easily, rewarding her. He lifted his head. "Now, let's define your fears. What exactly are you afraid of?"

"You know what I'm afraid of."

"Oh, yes, I know what you're afraid of. History repeating itself." He put his arm around her shoulder and guided her out of the room. "You know, my guess is your mother and father talked a lot but they never really said what they meant to each other. Your mother never said to your father, 'Please hold me, I'm afraid.' And your father never said to your mother, 'Do you love me for just me, myself? Would you love me if I weren't a writer?'"

She stared up at him. "Or," Luc said lightly, "he might have said something really important. Like . . . what's for dinner tonight?"

He smiled at her, an engaging grin. She was silent for a moment, registering his change in mood. Then, through laughter that was close to tears, she choked out the words, "You are a low, sneaking, double-dealing chauvinist."

He considered it and nodded in agreement. "I'm also a lousy cook."

"What makes you think I'm any better?"

"You've got to be better than I am," he said with heartfelt sincerity. "You couldn't be any worse. Let me do something more suited to my talents. Like doing the dishes."

And so she fixed dinner and he did the dishes.

Luc's entrance into her life was as simple—and as complicated—as that first meal together in her apartment. As the days and nights went by, he eased himself into her life. She was not accustomed to having someone around while she was working, but Luc understood that writing was a solitary process. He solved the problem by staying in bed mornings while she wrote.

"You don't need to make such a big sacrifice for me," she teased him that afternoon when he wandered out into the kitchen.

"No sacrifice is too great to insure the continued smooth production of copy by my favorite columnist."

"Do you really read my column, Luc?"

She was fixing their dinner, and he was engaged in his favorite occupation—watching her. She had her back to him, but he heard the cautious testing, the vulnerability in her voice. Filled with the need to wipe her insecurity away, he reached for her and turned her into his arms. "Of course I read your column, nitwit. Me and half the rest of America. I wouldn't miss it. What you write is damned interesting. How do you think you got to be a syndicated columnist anyway? For your good looks and sexy body?"

Her eyes blazed with pleasure. She stood on tiptoe and kissed him with a soul-stopping combination of gratitude and passion. An answering passion flared in him, and he deepened the kiss, probing her mouth with his tongue.

Dinner was delayed that evening.

The days settled into a routine. He had been right when he said sleeping late wasn't a sacrifice for him. His internal clock was set on a different time base than hers. He worked in the afternoon, she discovered. So she left him alone and went out to do library research or food shop in order to give him the privacy he needed. He was working on a book, she knew, and he had a deadline.

He spent several evenings at the play rehearsal, but one evening he came home with a gray face and said to her, "I'll have to stay away from the theater for a little while. I can't watch it anymore. It's too painful."

She didn't ask him what he meant. She simply opened her arms, and he walked into them.

Rana's life revolved into a wonderful pattern of work and pleasure. With Luc, she talked, and laughed, and learned to play. They did the traditional things and went to the top of the Empire State Building to look out over the city where they had met and to let the wind blow through their hair. One evening a week later, feeling smugly modern and up-to-date, they dined at Windows on the World on the one hundred and seventh floor of the World Trade Center. With the glass all around, and a view of New York City that was spectacular, she looked only at Luc. His brown hair was ruffled slightly from the October breeze, and his face had lost those lines of strain.

On some very special evenings they stayed home and sat on the couch and simply talked, discovering each other. But there was one topic they didn't discuss. They didn't discuss what would happen after October twenty-second.

A week before the opening night of the play, just after dinner, Rana went into the bedroom to dress and go out for the evening.

Luc frowned when she came out in a swirl of Arpège and a winter-white suit. The collarless jacket was short, fitted to her hips, and had four small buttons placed close together and low to expose the long, golden line of her throat and the valley between her breasts.

"Don't you have anything on under that thing?"

She did; it was a white satin camisole top with sequined spaghetti straps that clung to her body like a slip, its V neck cut so low that it didn't show above her jacket.

"I'm not sure that's any of your business," she said coolly.

"There's one way for me to find out."

The atmosphere turned frigid. "Is that a threat, Luc?"

He said in a lazy, silky voice, "You haven't considered my undressing you a threat—until now."

She said just as silkily, "You've always had my consent—until now."

170

The electric silence vibrated with animosity. Behind those narrowed eyes hooded with coffee-brown lashes, his mind was clicking away as he studied her, she knew that. But she didn't know what direction it was clicking in. "Where are you going?" he asked.

"To a fashion show for men's clothes," she said, her voice frosty. "I believe I mentioned it to you last night."

"I don't remember you mentioning it."

"Perhaps you were thinking about something else at the time. You had just come out of the tunnel."

They had devised a name for the intense state of concentration writing required. Luc had mentioned that he felt as if he were in a time tunnel when he began to write about the history of the West, and Rana had immediately recognized that she felt the same way when she wrote even though she didn't write about the past. They had laughed about it at the time and wondered if they should have a decompression chamber to cushion the shock of coming out into the real world.

He pushed himself up out of the blue velvet couch. "Mind if I go with you?"

She gazed at him steadily. "Yes, I do mind, Luc. If you go with me, I won't be able to concentrate on my impressions of the show. I'll be thinking instead about this quarrel and how you're interfering with my work and how much I resent that."

One dark-brown eyebrow climbed slowly upward. "Did I really say I wanted your honesty?" he murmured in a wry tone.

"Yes, you said that, Luc," she agreed, her voice slightly unsteady. "But like most people, you want honesty only if it doesn't hurt you."

"That's not true, Rana, and you know it." He hesitated and then said, "Don't go. Stay home and let's talk about this."

"Luc, I can't . . . can't get involved in an argument. I've got to go. I've been planning to attend this show for column material for two months, and I need every ounce of concentration while I'm there. I can't be thinking about you and me and what I feel for you while I'm trying to absorb a hundred sights and sounds and smells so I can recreate them on paper."

He said slowly, "I . . . can understand that." He opened his mouth as if he were going to say something more and then closed it.

His capitulation bothered her. It was as if she expected him to continue the argument, and when he didn't, she was thrown off-balance. She said, "I'll be late. Don't wait up."

"If you're going to work, I might as well go out, too." He rose with that lithe grace that always seemed to reach out and tug at her. "I'll probably drop by the play rehearsal and see how it's going." He walked around the couch to come to her, but as he leaned forward to kiss her, he looked at her closely and then pulled back. "I'd better not kiss you. I'll smudge your makeup."

She almost said, that's what it's for, but she didn't. But after she walked out of the door into the cool October night, she wished very much that she had. It was the first time they had parted without kissing good-bye.

The fashion show was in the Roosevelt Hotel in the ballroom. The male models smiled their plastic smiles or looked dark and broodingly sexy according to some master plan and paraded on a promenade especially designed for them down through the middle aisle and across the stage. Rana sat in the balcony and looked down on the glittery crowd below, struggling to absorb everything. The audience was a mixed bag: men and women who came to look and perhaps buy and who hid any excitement they felt under a bored exterior, would-be designers who were there to learn, and, directly below her, a segment of the press, photographers and reporters.

She found herself intrigued by the patter. Normally a meaningless repetition of the names of fabrics and a description of each garment, tonight's narrative was interspersed with interesting facts of the history of men's clothing. She turned her tape recorder on and continued to survey the crowd, listening to the words that spun in her head, trying to find phrases that would pinpoint and describe—and saw Phil. He sat about three rows back from the runway. He was with a woman, a blonde. From a distance Rana had no idea of her age. She could have been anywhere from twenty-five to fifty-five.

Then, as the show progressed, she forgot Phil. With each model's appearance, a bit more of the history of men's clothes was included. She found the entire thing fascinating and turned up the volume on her tape recorder to make sure she caught everything. As the show went on, she scribbled, adding written notes to detail her impressions.

On the way out, she found Phil at her elbow.

"Hello, Rana." He caught her arm and brought her to a standstill, studying her, taking in every detail of her clothing and that smooth, slim column of her throat with its eye-catching V of skin below. "You're looking . . . well."

"Thank you. So are you." She began to walk, faster this time, with Phil in tow. In her anxiety to escape him and the crowd, she bumped into one of the men who was evidently as anxious to get away as she was. The man turned. She recognized him instantly. He was one of the photographers who had been at Helen and Clem's party. In a movement as smooth as glass, the man brought his camera up, aimed, and focused. The click of the shutter told her he had caught her at close range with Phil holding her arm. "Nice to see you again, Rana O'Neill," he flung back over his shoulder at her and disappeared in the crowd.

She was furious. "I don't know how I got to be such hot copy," she complained to Phil, who had tightened his grip on her elbow and was helping her work her way to the elevator. Where was the blond woman he had been with at the show?

"I think it's your . . . liaison with Luc Garrett that has brought you your instant status as a celebrity."

"My . . . liaison?"

Phil gave her a cool look. "It's fairly common knowledge around town that he's moved in with you."

"I . . . see. I suppose I can expect to find that picture in tomorrow's paper under the heading, 'Has Rana O'Neill Ditched Lucas Garrett for a New Love?' "

"That's a distinct possibility," Phil said easily. There was a pause. The elevator reached the ground floor. Phil escorted her down the steps to the street entrance. Still holding her, he said, "I hope Garrett will understand. If he doesn't, I have a shoulder you can cry on."

Utterly astonished, she looked up at him. "Phil, I—you can't mean that."

"I do mean it, Rana," he said huskily, "and don't you forget it."

Impulsively, she put her hand on his arm. "Thank you, Phil, really. I . . . I'm sure it won't be necessary, but . . . I do appreciate it."

Touched by his offer, yet relieved to be leaving Phil behind, she ran out into the street and captured a cab on the first try.

When she got home, the silence and darkness of the apartment told her that Luc hadn't returned. She went into the office and sat down and began to write. She lost track of time, but she knew that several hours had gone by because she had the column almost finished when she heard the click of Luc's key in the lock.

They had an inviolate rule. No interruptions for idle talk. Rana knew Luc would see the light on in her office and stay away.

A few minutes later, feeling euphoric because she hadn't expected to complete her column until tomorrow, she got up and went to see where he had gone.

He had fixed coffee. The kitchen was warm with the aroma of it. His eyes distant, Luc sat at the snack bar turning a cup around in his hand.

She pulled a mug down from the cabinet and wondered what she should say. His mood seemed—odd. Was he still angry?

He said blandly, "How was the show?"

"Great. How was rehearsal?"

He grimaced. "Lousy."

174

She looked up at him, alarmed. "What's the matter?"

"Damned if I know." He ran a hand through his hair.

"It's probably very good. You're too close to it, too critical. Give it a rest, Luc."

"I don't have much choice, do I? Opening night is next Saturday." He sipped his coffee, then set his cup down and said in a carefully offhand voice, "Let's go into the living room and get comfortable. Bring your coffee and talk to me."

She looked at him and saw the tiredness around his eyes. "Maybe you should go to bed."

He looked up and caught her eyes with his. "Is that an invitation?"

She didn't know how to answer that. He seemed too disheartened to really mean what he said. "No," he murmured, "I didn't think it was. Well, my invitation still holds. Let's go in and sit on that couch." He hesitated, a strange look sliding over his face. "I won't have many more chances to get my share of use out of it, will I?"

She was still dealing with the pain of hearing him talk so casually about leaving her when she slid off the stool to follow him into the living room. When they stood together in front of the sofa, he took her coffee cup from her hand and set it down on the low table in front of him. She expected him to do as he usually did, sit down and pull her into his arms. He didn't. He stepped aside and slumped into the corner of one of the huge sectionals a long, aching distance away from her. Confused, she stood for a moment before she turned and sat down, struggling to hide her emotional turmoil.

"Anything interesting happen at the show?" he asked as casually as if everything were normal between them.

She opened her mouth to tell him about meeting Philip. But . . . something stopped her. His mood was strange, withdrawn. Suppose, after their altercation tonight, he was trying to find a way to tell her that he was no longer interested in staying with her? Her blood chilled. But if that was the case, the picture would give him a legitimate out . . . and save her pride. . . .

She forced herself to say in a cool tone, "It was rather well done. They included little tidbits about the historical evolution of men's clothes." Desperate to somehow get through this difficult moment, she plunged on. "For instance, that suit jacket you're wearing. Do you know why it has a buttonhole up there on the lapel where it serves absolutely no purpose?"

"Because the design was taken from the military uniforms worn during the Civil War. The uniforms buttoned up the front to the neck, and when the soldiers were off duty, they wore the flap open. The civilians liked the look and adapted it to their clothes, worthless buttons, buttonholes, and all."

"I should have known it wouldn't be a surprise to you," she said lightly.

He eased out of his jacket and tossed it on the back of the sofa between them. "The side vent was originally the slit where a gentleman's ceremonial sword handle protruded."

Luc's sleeve lay within easy reach. She ran her fingers over the buttons that had no buttonholes. "The buttons were once actually used to button back the cuff of the coat."

"And, according to legend, Frederick the Great or Napoleon, take your pick, left them there to prevent the soldiers from wiping their noses on their sleeves. Now," he said, his eyes taking on a strange gleam, "tell me what you learned about the vest."

Luc was wearing one, unbuttoned, a soft leather oxblood garment that fit close to his body. The vest was western in cut and color and a favorite of his. He wore it often around the apartment when he was writing.

She said, "It's a very shortened version of the gentleman's waistcoat, an inner garment that buttoned down the front and fell to the knees and was slit to the waist for more comfortable wearing. Like the vest of today, it had no sleeves."

"Exactly," he said and took off the vest. "Did you learn anything else?"

Had she thought he was tired? The tiredness had fallen away

like the clothes he was shedding, and in its place waves of sexual energy reached out to her.

"The tie," she said, her eyes never leaving his face, the love and desire rising inside her and burning like a fever, "was probably first used to hold the shirt and the collar together because, originally, they were separate." Luc wore a western tie with a slide clasp. "That particular one you're wearing might be considered a modern version of the cravat."

"Out West," Luc said, "cowboys trailing cattle wore colored bandannas for a very good reason, to cover their noses and keep the dust out."

Rana bent her head, acknowledging his area of expertise. When she raised her eyes, she saw that Luc was loosening his tie. He drew down the clasp and then, slowly, deliberately, pulled the tie out from under his collar. Silk slid against silk in a sensuous sound that made chills radiate over her flesh. Luc tossed the tie on the pile of clothes growing beside her.

"What else did you learn?" His fingers moved over his shirtfront.

She took a breath, feeling suddenly as if her lungs had forgotten how to function. "You men owe your uncomfortable starched collars to Beau Brummell. He was the dandy who liked a stiff cravat."

"Did he, indeed?" Luc's eyes were alive with laughter as his hands moved down along the line of his shirt fasteners. The snaps came free, one by one with a tiny pop, pop, pop, that echoed in the room.

Rana's hands shook with the effort it took to keep from reaching out and touching him. She clasped them in her lap. Luc obviously enjoyed tantalizing her, but he hadn't made a move toward her.

He sat up, pulled his shirt away from his pants, stripped it off, and added it to the growing pile on the back of the couch. "Do you have anything else to contribute to my education?" His eyes were lazily sensual, daring her to continue.

If he thought she was going to be the first to back down from

177

this titillating game, he had better think again. "Men's trou—"
At the first sound she uttered, Luc unfastened the buckle and
pulled the leather through his pant loops. Her voice caught in
her throat. She took a breath and tried again. "Men's trousers,"
she said with slow, husky emphasis, "are a fairly new addition
to a gentleman's wardrobe. Before the early eighteen hundreds,
men wore breeches, pants that fastened tightly either above or
below the knee much like our knickers, and paired them with
stockings that showed off the gentleman's well-formed calf."

Luc sat down and pulled off his boots in obvious preparation
for removing his pants. She swallowed and went on. "After the
early eighteen hundreds trousers were worn as informal daytime garments. They were"—Luc removed his socks and stood
up. She stumbled to a halt. "They were—"

He looked up, that dark roguish smile lifting his lips. "What
were they, Rana?"

He stepped out of his fawn-colored pants and tossed them on
top of his shirt.

She gazed at his long lean legs, the hard, attractive thighs
with their covering of curly hair, the curved calf muscles she
had once soaped. "Calf length," she managed to get out. "Pants
were calf length. Around the year 1825, the long trousers of
today came into general use—at least"—she choked on the
laughter that threatened to spill out—"most of the time." She
looked up at him, her eyes alive with delight.

Bare and golden and very male, stripped of everything except
the most basic garment, he sat down next to her. "Now," he
said, his voice soft with intensity, "if I tell you I have every
intention of finding out exactly what you're wearing underneath
that jacket, will you accuse me of threatening you in a voice
that would freeze a man's blood in his veins?"

"Oh, Luc," she whispered, "Luc." Her hands were no longer
in her control. They reached out to touch that warm, familiar
chest, to seek and find the delights hidden under the light covering of brown hair. "Please. I can't stand being distant from you.
Kiss me. I need you—"

He groaned a deep, heartfelt groan that seemed to come from the bottom of his soul and covered her mouth with his. His breathing quickened and he raised his head. His fingers moved to the buttons of her suit. The tiny cloth loops puzzled him at first, but in the next instant the top button came free—and the next—and the next—and the next.

Her jacket joined the pile of clothes. "You see," she whispered. "I *was* wearing something."

"This"—he inserted a finger under the tiny strap of the satiny top—"is not 'something.'" He let his finger travel down into the depths of the valley outlined by the satin and discovered the sweet fullness of her rounded curves. "This just barely misses being 'nothing.'" His hand traveled over her shoulder and around to the low back where he found the zipper that opened from top to bottom.

The zipper slid. "Umm, beautiful." He brushed aside the edges, and cool shivers raced over her skin from the contrast between the air and his warm hand. "You have a beautiful back, Rana O'Neill, have I ever told you that?"

His mouth began to make light love nibbles that robbed her of the power to think. "I don't think so. Most of your concentration has been focused on . . . my . . . front."

"A very serious oversight on my part. One I intend to remedy immediately."

He reached around under the camisole top and cupped one breast to hold her in place while his mouth traveled the length of her spine to the top of her skirt band. She trembled in anticipation, whispering for him to stop. He chuckled softly and pressed shivery kisses along the sensitive skin that lay close to the bone.

With Luc holding her as he was, she was helpless to do anything but quiver under his sensual caresses. She moved to free herself, to touch him, to tell him how much she adored him.

"No." His arms tightened around her bare waist and held her locked against his bare chest and hip. "Just enjoy yourself. Believe me"—his voice was a dark, velvety rasp—"I am."

179

When he had kissed and caressed every inch of her back and had her tingling with heated warmth, he nudged his hand under the side of the camisole top and pushed. The tiny straps fell off her shoulders and the camisole dropped in her lap. He added its shimmery beauty to the collection of clothes. Her skirt and hose followed in quick succession.

As he drew her bikini away, he kissed his way down her abdomen to the tops of her thighs and then lower, trailing stinging kisses and tiny love bites down the length of her silken leg to the sensitive skin around her ankle and the bottom of her sole.

He brushed his mouth over her toes, and she started in shock and surprise. "Luc!"

"Ticklish?" He lay down beside her, his underpants gone, his body warm and male and wonderful against hers.

In the time that followed, Luc kissed and caressed her with a new warmth, a new understanding, a tender possession that sent her soaring. And she pleasured him, listening to his murmured encouragement and indrawn breaths that signaled his delight, her deep satisfaction in pleasing him magnifying the pleasure he gave her. The weeks they had been together had taught them much about each other, and the time they had spent apart that evening had taught them more. He was hungry for her, and she was desperate for him, driven by a need that consumed her.

He seemed to know instinctively that she needed everything he could give. With his hands and mouth, he brought her to the brink again and again. Then, to heighten her pleasure, he cooled the flames, running his hands lightly over her body, soothing her, comforting her, murmuring to her to wait, wait, until, at last, her caresses drove him to the edge, and he could no longer leash the driving force of his passion. As if ordered by one mind, they came together in a storm of desire, entwined in that ultimate embrace of love.

She tried not to think of how few days there were left, but the number drummed in her brain. Three. There were three days

180

left until Luc's opening night. The sun was relentless, the moon equally so. Two. Then one.

The afternoon of opening night she was alone, working. Luc hadn't moved his dress clothes over to Rana's place, so he had gone back over to his own apartment to get ready and dress there. She had agreed to take a taxi alone to the theater and find her seat by herself. Luc would be tied up beforehand, greeting the cast, speaking with the director, going over any last-minute details with the producer.

And while she was working, the phone rang.

"Rana?"

If she had asked herself who she'd least like to hear from the day of Luc's opening night, Sam would have been high on the list. "What can I do for you?"

"Scuttlebutt has it Garrett's got a play opening on Forty-second Street. Anything to that?"

"A good newspaperman doesn't believe all he hears, you know that, Sam," she said, her voice casual, her heart beating in a rapid rhythm.

"No, but he tries to follow up on what he hears. The truth, Rana."

She sighed. "Yes, Luc has a play opening tonight on Forty-second Street."

"Rana, I want a column from you about it."

"Sam, we've been over this ground before. The answer is no."

There was a small, poignant silence. "I let you tell me no once before against my better judgment in deference to your obvious involvement with him. But this time I don't care how much you love the guy. I want a column about that play."

"Then hire a drama critic," she cried and slammed the phone down.

It rang almost immediately. She contemplated throwing it into the wall. Instead, she said into the receiver, "Sam, the answer is no and it's going to stay no until hell freezes over. Now get off my back."

"Hey." Luc's voice, his familiar, wonderful voice sounded in her ear. "What's the matter, honey?"

"Luc! I'm sorry." Her knees shook in reaction, and she gripped the table to steady herself. "I thought you were someone else."

"I hope so." He sounded amused. "I'd sure as hell hate to have you talk to me like that. Who's bugging you, sweetheart?"

"Nobody. It's nothing. How are you doing?"

"Great, if I could stop shaking. I'm afraid to shave myself."

"Don't be. The play will be wonderful, I'm sure of it."

"I hope you're right. I . . . just called to hear your voice. For luck."

She said ruefully, "And I yell into your ear like a shrew."

"Isn't Sam your connection at the syndicate?"

"Yes. Luc, you probably shouldn't be standing here talking to me. You should be holding your hand steady and shaving and—"

"He wants you to do a column about the play, doesn't he?"

She stood silent, wishing fervently that he didn't have a brain that put two and two together and got four like lightning.

"Doesn't he?" he repeated with a lethal softness in her ear that warned her not to lie to him.

"Yes. But I can't do it. You know I can't."

"Why not? Because you're sure it's going to be a bomb?"

"Luc, that's not the reason."

"I have no objection to your writing about the play. After all, every bit of publicity for the cast is a plus."

"Luc," she said through gritted teeth, "I don't want to write about you."

"Because you're afraid you can't be honest."

"Luc. Don't do this to me. Please."

She heard a sound, a breath of air expelled. Then in a light tone, "I'll see you at the theater, all right?"

"Yes, I'll see you there."

Because she had been so caught up in the thought that the beginning of the play meant the end of their love affair, she hadn't really thought about the play itself.

Now, she began to think about it. And worry.

She waited until the last possible moment to get ready. Then, as nervous as a cat, she rode to the theater and climbed out of the cab. She'd worn a daringly different jump suit in a shade of blue that made her eyes dark and silvery. The jump suit looked modest enough from the front and even had long sleeves, but when she turned around, a wide triangle of creamy skin was visible from her waist to the crisscross fastening at her nape.

There were people standing in the lobby; one or two of them recognized her. She nodded briskly and hurried past them to accept a program from the usher and be shown to her seat.

The lights dimmed; the play began. She sat tense, waiting. At first the audience was quiet. Then the coughing began, not a lot, but just enough to throw the actors off. The second act was worse, disintegrating minute by minute. By the end of the middle of the third act, the audience was very restless. A few got up and left.

She sat in her seat, her heart sinking to her toes.

She had agreed to meet Luc backstage. She wished she had told him she would go back to the apartment and wait for his call. But she couldn't leave. Once, long ago, he had asked her to hold his hand on this night. She was afraid he needed a much stronger medicine.

She threaded through the clutter of the backstage area, the smells of greasepaint and glue and electrical connections old and familiar. "Watch out for those cords," a stagehand warned her. "Mr. Garrett? I think they're holding the wake in the second room on the right."

She knocked on the door. A feminine voice, muffled, said, "Come in."

She opened the door. There were a half-dozen people crowded into the dressing room—but she saw only Luc, seated

183

in a large wicker chair, a glass in his hand—and the lead actress cuddled on his lap, the woman who had been with him that night in Tavern-on-the-Green.

Luc stared at her, his eyes going over her as if he didn't recognize her. "Here she is. My Fair Lady." His eyes were glittery. "Did you come back to join the victory celebration, sweetheart?"

She stared at him, feeling very alone—and very alien. She swallowed and took a step forward. It was then she saw the paper lying on the dressing table—folded back to the page with her picture on it. The publisher had held the photo for release on the same day as Luc's opening night—and run it on the same page.

"Well, tell us what you thought of it, Rana," Luc said. "You've had years of experience listening to your mother. You ought to have some very . . . succinct things to say."

The actress stretched up to kiss Luc on the cheek. The room reeled. She reached out, groping for something to hang on to. She found an arm, an arm clothed in a male suit jacket. She gathered herself and took her hand away from the male arm. She looked at Luc, the man she loved, and said, very slowly, very clearly, "I'll tell you exactly what I think. I think you should be home working on the rewrite instead of sitting there fondling the female lead." An electric silence vibrated in the room. Her head spinning, she turned.

"Rana." Luc's voice sounded desperate. She began to run. Behind her, there was a scuffling noise, a female protest, and Luc's voice turning the air purple with curses. "Rana."

She ran, thankful that because of those years with her father the rabbit warren of a backstage was as familiar to her as her own apartment. She raced down the steps, through the dark auditorium, and burst out into the street. A taxi cruised by, and whether the cabbie saw her bare back or her anguished face, she didn't know, but he stopped, and she climbed in just as Luc came pounding out of the theater.

She ordered herself not to turn and look at him, but it took all her willpower. She didn't weep in the taxi, but by the time she got to her apartment, she was shivering all over with shock and cold. She locked the door with the bolt and chain lock and went into the bathroom to turn on the shower hot and full.

She heard him at the door later, while she was huddling under the covers. He was trying to get in. He had his key, but the chain lock kept him out.

"Rana. Open this door." She put the pillow over her head, knowing he would go away eventually. And eventually, he did.

The next morning she sat at her computer and wrote the last column she would ever write about Lucas Garrett.

"Mr. Garrett has written a play," she wrote. "It is not a good play. Why? Because Mr. Garrett has forgotten the rules of fiction that made him a best-selling writer in the first place. Mr. Garrett has picked up the misconception that one form of fiction is different from another. Who was it who said, 'We go to the theater to worry'? Mr. Garrett, I watched your play last night, and I was not worried. Your characters were not in trouble. And when a playwright's characters are not in trouble, the playwright is. Remember James Bond, Mr. Garrett? He climbs a mountain and drives in three pitons to support his weight and keep him from falling to his death. The villian leans over the mountain and shoots away piton number one. Bond climbs again, and the villain shoots away piton number two. This time Bond rips his shoestring out of his boot and uses it to pull himself up the mountain. And piton number three, the only one holding James Bond on that mountain, is loose, Mr. Garrett, very loose.

"I recommend that you sit down and review the rules of fiction that you once knew. That knowledge put you among the ten best-selling authors in the Western world, Mr. Garrett. Apply those rules to your play. And then, in that quaint and favorite way we have of wishing stage folks luck, I suggest you go break your leg, Garrett."

The phone rang at regular intervals. At first, she simply didn't answer it. Then, in desperation, she put her answering machine on the line. That was worse. Because she ended up listening to him.

"Rana, forgive me. God, how can I tell you what an ass I've been in twenty seconds? That isn't long enough. You know it isn't long enough. Please answer my call. . . ."

And a few days later . . .

"I'm rewriting the play. You were right, of course, brilliant as always. Rana, listen to me. I—oh, damn it to hell! How the hell is a man supposed to talk to the woman he loves through a damn recorder!"

After that, she stopped listening to his messages.

The calls ceased abruptly. She read in the paper that the play was scheduled for reopening after Thanksgiving.

Another week passed. Snow fell, giving the city a child's Christmas card look. One morning she opened the paper and saw the reviews of Luc's play. "Garrett 'surprise package' hit of the Off-Broadway holiday season. Rewrite pulls Garrett play out of the doldrums. Best new Off-Broadway play in years, critic Richard Farris says. Rumor has it that a big-name producer has approached Garrett about doing a Broadway play next year."

She closed the paper with trembling hands, her spirits soaring. He had done it. He was a success.

She couldn't get a ticket to Luc's play. The house was sold out through March. Kris finally located one, through Steve, somehow, for a Wednesday night the week before Christmas.

She felt shaky as she dressed, but she knew she had to go.

Once in the darkened theater she was very glad she had had the courage to come. The play was wonderful, everything she had known it could be—and more. If he chose, Luc had a whole new career ahead of him.

At the end of the third act, she hurried up the aisle and

through the lobby. Outside the theater a hand on her elbow caught her and whirled her around to a dead stop.

She looked up into Luc's strained face. "Let go of me."

He shook his head. "Sorry. Not this time."

She thought about using a karate kick on him—or just a simple but effective knee to the . . .

"I wouldn't do it," he warned her. "Not if you plan on having any children."

"What are you talking about? What children? Let go of me."

Luc lifted his arm, and a car pulled away from the opposite curb and moved up in front of the theater. Luc opened the door. A young man whom Rana recognized at once was at the wheel. It was Steve.

She whirled on Luc, her face pale. "You set me up for this."

"Of course I did." None too gently, he pushed her into the backseat. "If you'd ever answer your phone, I wouldn't have had to resort to subterfuge. Driver," Luc said to a grinning Steve, "you know where to take us."

"Yes, sir."

"I'll get you for this, Garrett."

For the first time since he had grabbed her arm, he smiled. "I certainly hope so."

Silent with fury, her rebel body leaping to life under Luc's fingers, she turned her head to look out the window. When Steve pulled up in front of her apartment, she thought about breaking and running and discarded the idea as foolish. She wasn't a child.

Luc maintained his firm hold on her as they walked past the security guard and into the elevator. In the hallway outside her apartment, he said, very quietly, "Open the door."

To his surprise, she did it.

"Now close it." She complied again and then moved into the living room. He followed her. She turned. "Well? Say whatever it is you have to say and then get out."

He swung his head and looked around. "Where are those cubes you used to have?"

"Why? Do you intend to make a statue out of me again tonight?"

"Not quite. Where are they, Rana?"

It was curiosity more than anything that urged her to answer him. "I put them in the closet in my office."

He turned and went down the hallway. When he came back, he was carrying one in his arms. "These damn things are heavy."

"What are you going to do with them?"

"Put them to the most useful purpose they have ever served," he said, and dropped his burden in front of the door.

"What in the name of heaven are you doing, Garrett?"

"Locking the bad guys out and the good guys in. Old trick I learned writing westerns." He brought out cube number two and piled it on top of the first one. Cube number three went in front of the other two. They made a very impressive barricade.

Luc stepped back and viewed his work with a smile of satisfaction. Then he turned. Watching her, he walked toward her slowly. She stood her ground, not knowing whether to laugh or kiss him. He said in a soft, silky voice, "And the other thing I'm doing is getting the main character in trouble. I think those were your instructions, weren't they?"

"Luc—" caught between tears and laughter, she simply stared at him.

"Next step. Cut the guide rope."

She hadn't dressed up to go to the theater. She was wearing a simple black-and-red-striped sweater with a wide black belt at her waist and pants that flared over her hip and fit close to her ankle and boots to take her through the slush.

He reached for her—and under his hand, her belt fell away.

"Garrett—" her voice warned him, but she didn't move an inch away from him, "don't do anything you'll be sorry for."

"Oh, I won't. I intend to do something that will make me very happy indeed. Happier than I've been since that night you ran out on me."

"Ran out on you? Why, you overgrown cowboy, you have a

nerve saying I ran out on you. When you were sitting there with that bit of blond fluff all cuddled up in your lap. . . ."

His eyes glittered. "So it wasn't the remark about your mother that made you take off."

"Mother? I don't even remember what you said about my mother. All I remember is looking at you sitting there with another woman in your arms and wanting—really wanting to kill you." She reached out and looped her arms around his neck.

"And did it ever occur to you that that day will not rate high on my list of days to remember?"

"Because of the play—"

He shook his head. "The play was bad and that hurt, sure. But I had more on my mind than the play. You hadn't said one damn word about breaking that stupid agreement . . . and then that damn picture came out in the paper. I went crazy with jealousy. I wanted to strangle you."

"What?"

"Lift up your arms."

Without thinking she did as he asked, and her sweater was whisked off her body.

"Do you remember that afternoon I left the apartment? I didn't leave because my clothes were over there. I left because I couldn't stand the thought that you'd soon be reminding me my time was up and you wanted me to clear out."

"Luc! I thought you'd forgotten all about—"

"Oh, God. That's all I thought about all day. How could I ask you to let me stay when I promised you I'd go? I called you that afternoon, thinking you might say something, that you might admit that you were falling in love with me and wanted me to stay. When you didn't, I . . . I didn't know what to think. Until I saw that damn photo. Then I thought the worst. But after I cooled down a few days later and read the article more carefully, I realized that if the picture was taken the night of the fashion show, you definitely hadn't been with anyone that night but me—Why in hell are you wearing a bra?"

189

"There didn't seem to be any reason not to," she said dryly.

Deftly, he dealt with the clip and her bra followed her sweater. "Your safety rope's getting frayed, love."

"Luc," she murmured, swaying closer, his hands on her back sheer heaven, her body hungry for his touch, "do you think, honestly think, that we can survive"—she took a breath—"being married to each other?"

"You want my honest answer?" he said seriously, his mouth nuzzling under her hair.

"I wouldn't want any other kind."

"I don't think we can survive *not* being married to each other."

"But how can we know for sure?"

He smiled down at her, lifted her into his arms, and carried her into the bedroom. He laid her down on the bed, letting his eyes feast on the sight of her creamy curves. "Well, I tell you what. Let's try it for fifty years or so. And after that, if you don't like being married to me"—he laughed and pulled her close—"we'll go back to living together."

All-new
Candlelight
Newsletter

**An exceptional,
free offer awaits readers
of Dell's incomparable Candlelight Ecstasy and Supreme Romances.**

Subscribe to our all-new CANDLELIGHT NEWSLETTER
and you will receive—at absolutely no cost to you—exciting, ex-
clusive information about today's finest romance novels and nov-
elists. You'll be part of a select group to receive sneak previews of
upcoming Candlelight Romances, well in advance of publication.

You'll also go behind the scenes to "meet" our Ecstasy
and Supreme authors, learning firsthand where they get their
ideas and how they made it to the top. News of author appear-
ances and events will be detailed, as well. And contributions from
the Candlelight editor will give you the inside scoop on how she
makes her decisions about what to publish—and how *you* can try
your hand at writing an Ecstasy or Supreme.

You'll find all this and more in Dell's CANDLELIGHT
NEWSLETTER. And best of all, *it costs you nothing.* That's right!
It's Dell's way of thanking our loyal Candlelight readers and of
adding another dimension to your reading enjoyment.

Just fill out the coupon below, return it to us, and look forward to receiving the first of many CANDLELIGHT NEWS-
LETTERS—overflowing with the kind of excitement that only
enhances our romances!